Singularities

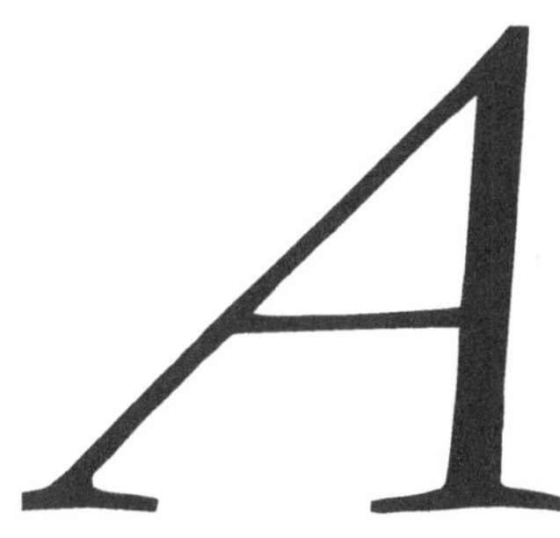

Holiday Story in the Cosmos

By a cosmic sailor—

or sailors?

A MULBERRY BARK BOOK
Published by
Mulberry Bark LLC

The characters and events portrayed in this book are fictitious but the loneliness is not.

For information contact Mulberry Bark LLC.
http://www.mulberrybarkpublishing.com

ISBN: 979-8-9855170-8-8

Also by the Author

Peter & Terpsi

Purpose of a Snowflake

Best Fudge This Side of the Milky Way

The Fixins

T-shirt in Winter

The Radio in the Galaxy's Heart

The Chasmwoe of Phantom Records

The Girl in the Bell Tower

The Wax Girl and the Copper Soldier

The Mask of Aubrey Clover

The Fabric

BOTCHO, IN LOVE WITH A HEADSTONE

For the lonely ones

"I'm so unwanted on this planet even gravity doesn't hold me." ~ An astronaut

"Everyone is a reminder of my loneliness—another one I don't belong with." ~ A visitor to Earth

Please, warm yourself by the pagefire, where a holiday story is crackling by the shore…

An astronaut will soon set sail for the open cosmos, on a long journey into uncharted celestial sea, all by his lonesome, trillions of miles away from women, mating, friendship and romance. *An* astronaut, any generic astronaut, really, since the public only sees the generic *spacesuit*, not the actual journeyer inside with big dreams, bigger fears, a girl he loves, a holiday wish, and a secret too strange to admit to anyone. That real being never gets interviewed, only his image.

So, the public imagines a brave, iconic *spacesuit* will be voyaging in the spacecraft equivalent of a rowboat, on his expedition to a "new" world (new to humans, old to its inhabitants, if it has inhabitants). The star sailor's blue eyes will be the first human eyes to view this foreign world up close.

Two lightyears away, a star system, closer to Earth than the Alpha Centauri system, was discovered a few years earlier, "hiding" in the constellation Sagittarius, where the Milky Way's heart is also tucked.

"Listen, no one was looking in her direction," the astronaut said at a press conference, explaining how he found "her."

In 1977, decades ago, a radio signal was received, the famous "Wow! Signal," that also came from the direction of Sagittarius, and many believed, some still believe, it was extraterrestrial in origin. "But there are other explanations for the signal, unfortunately," the astronaut once confessed.

Fortunately, in this newly discovered star system, there might be a habitable planet, a "new" world, and who knows what else. The "what else" has mostly everyone excited (or frightened of aliens, or ready to exploit aliens, or bored because so far none of this has lived up to Hollywood sci-fi fantasies).

Even the most skeptical are curious: what—or who?—will the starfarer discover out there in the "deep" end of cosmic ocean? "*Deep* end of cosmic ocean is just a phrase, since *deep* is relative in space," the astronaut explained at the same press conference.

This noble explorer will be the first human to break free from the sun's gravitational pull. Like a turtle hatchling daring the dangerous journey into the ocean, his travels will take him far beyond Earth's shoreline, far beyond his nest (the solar system). But unlike a child who goes away to college, planning on making trips back home on occasion, the star sailor will never return to Earth, not even for the holidays; no more jelly doughnuts and roasted vegetables from Earth. The astronaut has a one-way "ticket." Everyone, strangers and family and colleagues and journalists, tells him, "Hope bad weather doesn't stop your trip."

Unbelievably, the star traveler might make first contact with beings from the other world if the distant world turns out to be populated; he might encounter caravans along a celestial "Silk Road," where interstellar traders exchange spices, goods, star maps, and knowledge from their home planets. Someday, when Earth kids are attending intergalactic schools, studying the chemistry and evolution of Planet Q, and humans are holiday-ing and ice skating on the purple pond of some planet X, his name might be a synonym for voyager, like Magellan and Polo. He'll surely be written about in Earth's history books as the Columbus of the Cosmos; his name might even be immortalized in some Galactic Encyclopedia.

Really everyone on Earth already knows of the modern Space Age "hero," former Navy pilot/captain, Top Gun, "true Americana" (a melting pot of Greek, Italian, Jewish, English, African, Native American genes), an astronaut/radio astronomer/alientologist with a reputation as a "playboy." In the hypersonic X-309 jet, the hotshot pilot broke the airspeed record for fastest manned flight: Mach 7 (seven times the speed of Beethoven reaching your ear). He is now captain of Mass Spacecraft's elite crew of astronauts like the Navy Seals. "Sexy nerd," so labels the press. One women's webzine said the astronaut looks like one of the finer things in life: gorgeous, rich, served with wine. "Colonel Cute," "Commander of Cool," "Astrohaut." Social media tags. Named by *Lorisel* magazine as The Sexiest Man on Two Worlds, back when he did the Mars mission, and his mother, the publicist, had a "priceless" connection with *Lorisel.* Thanks to his publicist, Earth's populace knows a little about the man inside the spacesuit, or a little about his persona anyway; no one knows his secret, not even his mother. The astronaut has political pedigree (his granddad a U.S. Congressman) and a heritage from the stars (of the Walk of Fame variety). Born in the ice of Antarctica, he was raised in the lusty sunshine of California, but some claim the scientist's icy personality never thawed, and in fact, has only become colder. He has an "okay body," wrote a hateful, Internet critic, who mentioned the astronaut's slightly "doughy" stomach formed by a junk-food addiction (the rocketeer is also a doughnuteer, chocolateer, pizzateer, etc.). His mother/publicist boasts that the astronaut is currently the most famous human in the world. But the least comprehended. A telephoto lens cannot peer deeply into the star. Even telescopes the astronomer uses to understand the galaxy's heart must "see" beyond the visible range to probe the Milky Way's core and its secrets. But what matters to the public is that the astronaut has a stellar face, forty years old and untouched by weathering (thanks to airbrushing), a "stellar" face that sells magazines, publicity b.s., and this risky voyage—that smile of his can sell anything, even the belief that he's happy. The masses like an astronaut, or don't like him, because of his "sexy" tousled black hair, 1970's-style with sideburns, and his "gorgeous" blue eyes, and his "perfect" teeth, except for one hole in a molar created by a love of Jack 9 gum, the decay hidden by tooth-like veneer—a scandal! revealed by his dentist to a tabloid Internet site.

Two weeks ago, at another press conference, in a generic room as businesslike as staplers and filing cabinets, a reporter asked, to get a tasty scoop more sellable than former scoops, "Will there be any special gal in the audience, waving farewell to you?"

Laughing, *an* astronaut snapped, "If there was, would I be leaving?"

Everyone roared with laughter. At these press events, the astronaut often answers, or avoids?, questions with wit and humor. The heroic spacesuit doesn't require trivialities such as a special gal, a fact which all the seated reporters agreed on with their shared laughter and wink-winks and nudge-nudges that said, "The Don Juan has too many *non*-special ones to take advantage of before he leaves Earth. After all, he's about to travel trillions of miles away from sex."

"Truthfully, I'm more concerned about being lightyears away from chocolate," he joked into the press conference mic, contradicting his reputation as "icy," which he does sometimes in his lectures, too, like when he describes the galaxy as a "carousel"—those kind of childish comments make the Top Gun seem more like a toy gun.

Absurdly trillions of miles away from the hope of mating, so the space agency is allegedly supplying the astronaut with a pretty sexbot (a detail about the historical mission "leaked" to the tabloids, or fabricated by them).

Unfortunately, no, no special gal waiting to kiss the sailor goodbye. No special gal to name his ship after. No special gal wanting to give him one last Christmas or Hanukkah present, waiting to share one last holiday meal together.

But numerous groupies, famous and non-famous, are willing to spend the historical night with the astronaut's "okay" body and stellar legacy at the Starlight Motel. At this seaside sleaze pad with cold damp walls, the beds shake during launches, which creates the illusion that trysts are Earth rocking, and might the groupie, afterwards, have his wallet, since he won't be needing it out there in space?

Is no one interested in the radio astronomer's work—his career-long work, his life-long obsession—on singularities, and the black hole, the possible singularity, in the Milky Way's heart emitting radio waves? The scientist tries to get the public excited by this astrophysical concept: a *singularity* is a cosmic "rabbit hole," a possible Wonderland of strangeness, where no known human has ever voyaged, where all conceptions of time and space completely break down. What goes on there???? Where does the "tunnel" lead? No one knows for sure, and that's what gives scientists' goose bumps. The astronomer has studied different scientific hypotheses (Planck stars and gravastars and "fuzzballs"…) and science fiction hypotheses (time portals, alternate universes, Heaven…).

So, who knows what is inside a singularity, but people know the astronaut's chest is tan and flat from a lifetime of beach lounging with hardback books and veggie-hummus tacos, leisurely sailing and swimming and snorkeling, and sunbathing with various beauties of all shades all over the globe. The public knows those details thanks to paparazzi who always seem to be tipped off to the astronaut's exact whereabouts (his mother's a publicist, go figure). Thanks to nosiness, everyone and their mother has seen the scientist's bare chest—the scientist's—bare, hair-shaved-off chest, either from those "revealing" beach photos or from all the news clips of him with electrodes taped over his hidden heart, undergoing tough experiments for space exploration, pictures which have been turned into "funny" GIFs posted on social media.

Those questioned as experts on the star scientist are women who claim to have shared a smidge of nighttime with his body, and colleagues who have shared a few hours with his informative side which anyone could meet in a science journal. Colleagues' descriptions of him vary so contradictorily they offer the public no clear-cut conclusion about the astronaut's personality—"pompous," "pleasant," "serious," "funny." One male coworker criticized, "You could put a tray filled with water in his hands and make ice cubes." Yet a female coworker countered, "He's as warm as your grandma." "Whoever said that must not have gone to bed yet with Mr. Mach 7," one of the alleged shareholders of his nights retorted. One colleague said, "Mars is the lovely gem no woman can ever compete with in the astronaut's heart." The astronaut has never responded to anything said about him publicly.

His bank account stats and the size of his "harem" are the aspects of his personal life the public is most interested in exploring.

Even so, like a public servant, the scientist is open about his scientific finds, such as his discovery of the new world and his research on singularities, but he is as locked as a diary about his personal life (hence the word *personal*). His mystique is a product of his lack of sharing information and the public's lack of caring to uncover important information like secrets, the kind of info that IDs someone more than name, age, occupation. The captain's stature as Hero is un-probed and validated by his image on cereal boxes. No one has dug out his boarded soul.

Mostly everyone knows the brave spacesuit has forgone numerous holidays to subject himself to numerous experimental tests for space exploration, although he did become the first human to eat *sufganiyot* (holiday jelly doughnuts) on another world, where he was docked in a spaceboat, during Hanukkah a few years earlier; the doughnuts were made for the starship captain by, fittingly, Donuts from Outer Space!

Undaunted, *an* astronaut has spent months in arctic seclusion, pushing the limits on how much coldness and pressure a human can endure, how much speed a person can tolerate, how much strain a heart can withstand…*how much isolation?*

So many know the naval captain has "the moon" in his logbook. He was the first human to taste "moon water," brought back as ice from Earth's moon, purified, and sipped on live TV at a Mass press conference. He joked he might turn into a superhero like LunarMan, like Peter Parker transforming into Spiderman after being bitten by a radioactive spider. "Someone call Los Angeles and tell them this is what water should taste like," the astronaut grinned with his so-called "charmcasm," charming sarcasm. Mass Spacecraft and the astronaut were both criticized for the "crazy little moon water stunt," as his dad, Jessie, labeled it.

Everyone knows the rocketeer was the first man to leave a bootprint on another planet's moon (Mars' Phobos), during Earth's Christmas season a few years past when he ate the jelly doughnuts. He was the first to toss a baseball on this moon. The event was immortalized through a photograph by a crewmate. The photo was reproduced millions of times to become decoration on kids' playhouse walls, dorm room walls, professors' office doors, Mass Spacecraft's billboards, an all-female baseball team's locker room wall, and his father's dartboard ("to be funny"). (There were rumors that the astronaut lost his marbles on Phobos, saw "strange" sightings, and that was why he didn't get the Venus mission, but a "crazy" man is just right for this "crazy" mission.)

Of course, those gimmicks *might* have secured the astronaut a line or two in history books, but so far in life, the "obsessively" ambitious and "fanatically" driven astronaut is not yet historical, not cemented in the books (anyone could break his Mach 7 speed record at any time). Many have been famous in the past, their images plastered on every sellable thing from posters to shoes, but now their names and faces are forgotten and commercially worthless, a fact which his publicity-generating mother constantly reminds clients, including her son.

"Finally, are you ready to leave Mother Earth behind?" *a* reporter once asked, prying for information that could sell his newspaper.

"To be frank, she's never been much of a mother to me," the astronaut laughed. "No, I'm not leaving her behind. In a way, I'm towing her into the future."

"Ha," the reporter laughed too, "but you can't tow our beautiful mountains and our seas and all the gorgeous Earth women to outer space with you. Won't you miss all that?"

Irritated obviously, the astronaut quipped, "I'll especially miss these press conferences."

"So, how are you feeling about exploring the universe?" another reporter asked.

The astronaut answered, "Imagine how *space* is feeling, about to be explored by a species with a brutal track record of violence and intolerance for differences. Earth is surely seen as the galaxy's 'bad part of town.' There may be all sorts of interplanetary travel restrictions against trips to Terra, and that's why no one visits us. So, perhaps this 'new' planet is intent on minding its solitude and doesn't want a visitor, especially a boorish Earthling, upsetting its peaceful landscape."

And when asked why he is going on the "suicide voyage," the astronaut said with a voice that never reveals anything going on inside him, "To seek out new life ... to boldly go where no one has gone before." Of course, the *Star Trek* line garnered headlines. He added, "I'm going on the mission to get a rock from another planet to add to my rock collection."

Laughs all around.

"Eee, no, it's not a voyage to death but to life." He quickly changed faces and tones, took off the wittyman mask and put on the mask of scientist, saying like a prophet, "Earth is like a sandcastle, surrounded by the rough, galactic sea, yet many cling to the comforting illusion of its permanence. Spacecrafts are modern boats, so humans can now sail to new islands in the cosmic ocean. It's time to expand the region of our planetary zip code before it's too late." A sobering yet noble, scientific answer that gave the masses exactly what they want—a Space Age savior, who promises a forever home in the stars, immortality in the heavens if not Heaven, and if not for each individual, at least for the entire human species, who will be saved from Earth's eventual destruction on an interstellar ark.

The public knows those publicized facts about *an* astronaut.

No one knows that engraved on the back of the star sailor's brass, antique compass are these words from Edith Södergran's poem "On Foot I had to Cross the Solar System":

"Somewhere in space hangs my heart,
shaking in the void"

The public doesn't see beating inside that sterile "futuristic" spacesuit is his old-fashioned heart's secret wish: to land on *her* planet. This astronaut might go madcap and abandon his historical billion-dollar mission if it turns out to be in the wrong direction, and set whatever course leads to *her*. Won't he?

Did any of those great voyagers of the past secretly share a similar wish that propelled their desire to travel, far and wide, to find *her?* The one *her* that seemed impossible to find on their own world, as if the environment of their world had never been quite right to evolve unique *her*, a being formed of starshine and an unnamable unfathomable element, that one special ingredient missing from all Earthlings—the gene Z that the ruthless nature of Earth would never select for. The Earthly bureaucratic environment has begun its own "natural selection," where traits are "selected for by the bureaucracy" through the process of firing and hiring; he senses her traits of sensitivity, non-conformity, and generosity would go extinct in an office.

So, yes, everyone *knows of* the hotshot astronaut, but no one knows he deeply yearns to leave Earth, except for those intuitive enough to read secrets by the light of empathy: The star sailor would paddle straight into a singularity, following intuition to find *her*, sensing her planet, her world, is deep inside the rabbit hole.

On the astronaut's planet, it's a time where old technologies, such as houses and robots, have been renovated, some for the betterment of humankind (solar-powered houses) and some for the deterioration (sexbots, which will eventually make romance extinct).

Not much else has changed on the pale blue world in centuries…

Loneliness has not been universally cured.

Youthful hearts are frowned upon.

Lying trumps truth.

Offcast concepts like telepathy, reincarnation, Nessie, destiny, immortality, and celestial matchmakers are viewed as unreal…

Verily, hate, prejudice, and war are still realities.

Entrance passes into cliques include current slang, fashions, and good looks (all throughout school, the astronaut was never accepted into any clique, and as a young boy he often wore snorkel fins and diving mask around town as the quintessential eccentric genius).

Ill-behaved money has not been eradicated and neither have the barriers and isolation it creates.

Sex, greed, fear, lust, and ego are still the primary decision makers.

Really it is not a world suitable for the *her*, not a world where phantastic gene Z can thrive, except maybe during the joyous, kind, whimsical season known as the Holidays.

Even so, despite humanity's lack of social and emotional improvements, humans have made advances in space exploration in The Space Age of Discovery.

And one such achievement in space travel is an experimental spacecraft (the fastest man-made object). After Earth makes one twirl from now to twenty-four hours later, the spaceship will launch the astronaut into permanent history, or death, or both if the spacecraft malfunctions. After one last Earth sunrise and sunset, the "well-known" astronaut will set out on the long solo journey which will answer that question—*how much isolation?* If weather permits, his trek to the faraway planet will set sail tomorrow at 9.p.m., Pacific Time, Terra (Earth) Time, December 20.

Launchpad 1 on Rocket Peninsula, across the cold nighttime waters of the Pacific Ocean, is where the experimental starship is pointed toward the unknown and awaiting its pilot. But for now, its high-tech body, mated to metal scaffolding, is getting old-timey rained on, and so is everyone working on and awaiting the historic liftoff.

The astronaut's spacecamper doesn't have a hearth, but like any RV ("spacebago," as the media calls it), the captain's cabin is equipped with a helm/sitting area for steering (he tried to convince the engineers to install an old timey ship's wheel but that was labeled "impractical" for the small "rowboat"). The public is interested in these facts about a spaceboat. The starcraft's quarters are brown like an old-fashioned ship deck, a color found agreeable by the astronaut; other colors made him nauseous when viewed for long periods of time. The spaceboat also has a fitness area, "kitchen," and "bathroom" (no bath, just rinseless shampoo and soap). On an upright stasis chamber, the astronaut will sleep even when he's not in stasis. He surely will miss that quaint bed and breakfast close by Lake Tahoe, Chocolate Truffle Inn, its plush beds with cloud billowy covers, fireplace in each suite, chocolate chip pancakes, and grandma-type innkeeper. The spacecamper's fitness area includes a foldable treadmill, which provides a screen with a hundred different scenes from Earth, in case the homesick astronaut wants to jog on the Chicago Riverwalk, or hike snowy Everest, or swim Cherry Lake outside Chocolate Truffle Inn, or climb flower-dappled Pomcasión Hill in Pyatha, or stroll the apple orchard close to his undergrad alma mater "Swell Ol' Goldell" in the autumn-scenic town of Biskatine. The workout station also includes a virtual reality headset, which offers opportunities to "play ball" in the Major Leagues, or ballroom dance (with a virtual partner), or light a menorah, or even build a snowman, all by himself.

Limits on cargo load, the mass of sustenance and equipment and pilot, is why the trip has to be solo. No room for anyone else, yet room for the treadmill to keep the lone heart in shape. Mass Spacecraft is more willing to sacrifice one person—a martyr, a hero!—as opposed to an entire crew for a mission that just might go down in history as the Titanic of space travel—"Ice rings, straight ahead!" No lifeboats, no parachutes, no crewmates, no chance to escape by ejecting from the cockpit, just one sailor and a small ship voyaging the universe in search of a home…and *her*? Will she leave the lights on for him?

The public knows that Mass Spacecraft, subsidiary of U.S. megacorporation Mass Enterprises, put the first humans in orbit around Venus in a blimp-like ship fit for The Jetsons, in "friendly" competition with other space agencies and countries like Russia's 9, Japan's Hakudo Maru, Europe's Aristarchus. The scope of the technology didn't shock the public as much as how quickly it developed. In the 1950s, alongside NASA, Mass worked on putting the first astronauts in space through the Aerodactyl project. Thanks to the work of pioneers like aeronautical engineer Gershom Blagonravov, Rock-It CEO Joe Chaikin, astrophysicist Harold Perchinky, and astronauts like Jaine Viatricibus and Peter Lieberman further advances in space exploration were possible. Thanks to sci-fi writers like Taggart Smythe, Octavia Butler, and Sidereus Sterling too. For years, Mass configured an ultra-fast, ultra-light, off-planet vehicle, capable of long-term and long-distance exploration and, oh yeah, protecting a human from risks associated with space voyaging—

can't have astronauts dying and ruining Mass Spacecraft's reputation as a "family company."

Mass Spacecraft reports these kinds of missions will make possible further deep space exploration (interplanetary arks) and future human colonization of other worlds. Mostly everyone is seemingly excited by the prospect of new homes (time to put up the mansions, trailers, white picket fences, and "No Trespassing" signs on Zenon). Plus, these missions will make copious amounts of money for Mass Spacecraft (although they didn't admit that as their purpose publicly). Mass Spacecraft may very well be like the European empires of The Age of Discovery interested in conquering more than exploring, willing to exploit and subjugate natives for profit. How long before extraterrestrial slaves are forced to mine all the discoveries—commodities—stolen from their planets to be sold on Earth, just like African slaves toiled in tobacco fields and sugar plantations in the Americas, so the Europeans could enjoy the products of slave labor? These kinds of cynical thoughts about humanity and space exploration have never made the scientist completely popular with his colleagues or the public.

After visiting Earth's neighbors like Saturn and Neptune, who have presumably never turned on a lighthouse for galactic seafarers to dock, the modern mariner will go into cold stasis and sleep in the darkness of immense space, missing out on many holidays and dates. The new world will take approximately thirty years to reach. The public enjoys these facts about space travel too. During this part of the voyage, the sailor's vitals will be monitored by a computer, which is not any drabber a fate than being under the care of an emotionless doctor; at least the computer has a valid excuse for lack of emotions—it wasn't made with any. At a publicity soiree, Mass Spacecraft boasted that during stasis tests the astronaut was capable of dreaming, so at least the long-distance traveler will have countless dreams for companionship. He will be like a baby in the womb, possibly asleep until arrival. But even though stasis is generous with dreams, the process is not kind about aging. While aging will be slowed, once out of stasis, cellular processes will make up for "lost time" by accelerating, which means when the astronaut returned to Earth, he would quickly age to make up for "lost years" (by then, he would be one hundred years old). It was his decision for the journey to be a one-way trip. The astronaut volunteered for the expedition. Mass Spacecraft made sure the public knew that too, so Mass wouldn't look heartless for sending a man to die, alone, in space, with only radio communication as a connection to his home world, for a mission that could be undertaken by a robot, although a robot wouldn't generate as much publicity or give the public a hero. After the mission, astronaut and spaceboat will continue to drift in galactic territory uncharted by humans, even long after engine and body die, in a starry graveyard (the captain goes down with his ship), unless…the new world turns out to be hospitable, in which case, the interstellar hobo would land and celebrate his seventieth birthday and the holiday season, alone?, on another planet. Or will he ditch his plans and head where intuition takes him?

For the moments out of stasis, the astronaut will be supplied with food to last, and hopefully curiosity too. His tablet will have enough power to maintain a long life. The tablet will be used for keeping a log and journal and for playing chess and Asteroids and other games against the computer. Much research and effort went into designing the explorer's food supply, not exactly warm hearty meals from the hearth but sustenance which comes in packages of dried food and thin melt-on-the-tongue strips that offer a day's worth of calories and nutrients. The spaceboat only has so much room for rations and only three dozen candy bars for possibly 22,000 days in space, so eat those Mr. Goodyums judiciously. Plus, food and its nutrients degrade with time, but the scientists at Mass were able to overcome obstacles against nutrition for man's unquenching quest to explore new worlds, even though those obstacles have never been surmounted for homelessness and starvation on Earth.

The astronaut will also have a library-size collection of books: philosophy, mineralogy, cartography, ancient languages, codes and systems of numerations, and Ag Clave's book of love poems, *Silk Mint*—these facts about the mission were reported but not found as interesting as the ship's schematics. Sometimes, a reporter looking for "fun tidbits" might ask a question like "What books are you taking with you?" "The Boy Scout's Guide to the Milky Way." More laughs, more fans, more headlines the lie garnered. Would *she* feel anything from Earthling love poetry? The books are downloaded on a device the size of a 5x7 picture frame, along with a plethora of movies, TV shows, and music. The astronaut can sail the stars with song, read Jules Verne with Neptune outside the porthole, and voyage to new worlds, while hearing Rod Serling say, "You've just entered *The Twilight Zone*." Plus, he'll have his guitar, clarinet, and keyboard that folds into a bulkhead, so he can be the first human to write a song inspired by the view from another solar system. But who will he sing it to? Will he be the Christmas caroler in the stars?

The public wants to know what the star sailor plans to do with his last twenty-four hours on Earth, not necessarily because they really want to know the astronaut (no more than they want to know what occurs in the *cores* of nighttime stars, since enjoying their prettiness doesn't require comprehension of their being), but many desire spicy details to vicariously spice up their own lives. Many people enjoy contemplating how they would spend *their* last day on Earth, which is really a search for an answer to this question, "What is the one thing, place, moment, or activity you most relish from this planet, or who is the one soul you most cherish? If you had but one hour left to live, who would you spend it with?" The astronaut always shrugs away the question, so a news anchor, in the voice of normality, answered for him, "I'm sure the world's most famous astronaut is spending his last time on Earth *at home with his family* like any of us would do, especially during the holiday season."

The unkind winter night seemingly has one goal: to slowly drain all rain from the sky by beginning with a weepy drizzle that culminates with a passionate storm—a storm that might postpone the historic mission. It's already been postponed twice. For now, the air is more wet with mist than full-fledged pearls of raindrops, but the holiday sky might go all out tonight and decorate Earth with snowflakes.

In this icy weather, the astronaut has something to do before he departs for his celestial cruise across the cosmos. Magellan of the Milky Way travels by jet ski, off the U.S.'s west coast in Burgundy Falls. Like mist over a frozen lake, paths of fog hover over the black sea. Over these white clouds, sea stones stick up here and there. Nebulous mist is a ghostly curtain across the beach shore, as the watercraft bumps along rough waves like a planetary rover over gravel. Effervescent milky crests rise over the sailor's bare feet. Loose water splatters everywhere from sky and sea. Yeti-powerful, the world's fastest jet ski, racecar-green, is shaped like a track runner's shoe but capable of running much faster than human feet.

The former test pilot has traveled faster than the thunder, which growls like some beast in the jungle of damp nighttime. In his experimental spacecraft, he'll almost achieve his boyhood dream: to catch up to the speed of lightning, to go where only light can travel.

For now, the astronaut is not wearing his iconic spacesuit, the colors of snow and sunshine; instead, the explorer is uniformed for diving: scuba tank strapped on his back, transparent eyemask covering his famous eyes, tubings and gauges and latches everywhere. A flashlight, mounted atop his cold-raw hand, is wrapped in a black strap for securing the light. His other hand controls the throttle lever. The astronaut is going to take one last dive beneath *this* world's surface—hoping to encounter *her* again in the sea?

An odd vision pushes into his walled mind: Inhospitable waves assault *something*…what is it the water is attacking? Some kind of midnight-blue cloth? A cloak? A wizard? The odd vision has to maneuver around other bulky thoughts about equations and etc., which are taking up a lot of space in the scientist's smart head, so he can't make out all the details of the fanciful cloak and therefore doesn't understand what he's seeing in his mind's eye.

Surely, cold-and-flu syrup created that loopy thought.

Through water-splashed goggles, he sees:

In the hostile ocean stand two peaceful rocks that are married, so says the legend of The Wedded Islets. The married rocks look to have been standing since the birth of Earth, having weathered all the planet's catastrophes with scars to prove it. Starboard stands the husband rock, who is taller, stonier, a prominent figure, an immaculate rectangular monolith, almost entirely smooth (he has gashes and scars too), while the shy wife rock, portside, is shorter, softer, mossier, and oddly shaped, too odd to be described with Earthly words. On sight, who would suppose the ancient pillars are married? Such an expanse of sea separates them, the entire night sky reflecting in the waters between them, they appear as two isolated
islets.

When *she* made her trip to Earth, did she see the rocks as married?

Yes, intuition whispers.

So, she did visit Earth? That was *her*?

The scientist shakes off the thought, not going to listen to any "answers," too crazy. Clutching the bike's handles, the starsurfer steers the seacraft through wild water and does a wheelie just for the fun of it—he'll never swim, surf, or sail Earth's seas again.

Above the old connubial stones, one lone star looks like a dot above a little "i," playing hide-and-seek in clouds. Some folks view the constellation Sagittarius as an "archer," but romantic types see the star formation as Cupid with a bow and arrow, maybe pointed at the galaxy's heart. Part of the constellation is referred to as "the teapot," whose spout billows out the Milky Way. Is *Yuè Lao*, the old lunar matchmaker god in charge of marriages, is he sitting on the crescent moon, swaying his bare feet in cosmic sea, sipping milky celestial tea, and crafting a plan with Cosmic Cupid to bring the astronaut and *her* together? Legend says *Yuè Lao* unites all predestined couples with the red thread of fate, attaching one end of the invisible string to each soulmate, maybe at the very birth of the souls (fresh from being made for each other by a divine tailor), and the romantic red thread may become tangled, stretched, hidden, and forgotten across lifetimes and galaxies and wrong relationships, but never torn through all eternity.

Aside from that charming image, the drizzly night looks sick, gray, shivering, pre-stormy like asking someone to take it home and nurse it with warm starlight, and so does the astronaut. He's enduring a cold: sore throat, headache, mild fever, not-so-mild general aches, and that strange sickness feeling of freezing while hot with fever. Ain't that a fine how-do-ya do—to get so sick right before the big mission.

Medicine, hospital *care*, that's another thing still not perfected on the pale blue planet.

Another odd vision makes it way around the explorer's other thoughts to come to the forefront of his crammed mind: a vision of a little egg-shaped sphere? A Neptune-blue orb? It looks like a mini planet, made of glass?, dappled in water droplets with a thin red…*river?* running around it? This shiny orb with red equator is important, he senses. It's being put inside a protective pouch with drawstring like a pouch from a mythological epic about dragons and faeries and elves.

His brain must be in a flu fog, or getting jarred by the rough ride, which is knocking loose oddball thoughts, the kind that isolated him in childhood as a misfit, the kind that the scientist has tried in adulthood to keep under logic's lock and key—so, he won't descend into madness! Too many boyhood days were wasted on searching for Hobbit-holes, and digging in sand to Alice's Wonderland, and diving for sunken treasure chests, and making little bootprints in Antarctic ice, searching for Santa's house (although everyone knows Santa Claus lives on the

North Pole, and Santa *Gloom* lives on the South Pole, where he mines coal for those on Santa Claus's naughty list).

The rabid ocean laps at the sailor with dozens of furious watery tongues like a foaming-at-the-mouth beast, as if trying to swallow the mariner into the salty abyss. But the married stones stand firm in churlish sea, whose gruff waves are unable to reach the sky, incapable of jarring the stars or any homes or beings *out there.*

Thunder is as loud as a chorus of rowdy drunks at a bar.

Getting slung around by ferocious waves, the astronaut looks through the misty space between the married pebbly pair, where stars slowly pass through the night cycle, the constellations robed in fog, the entire universe cloaked in mystery, waiting to be unmasked by him. Some spiritual types claim we're all actors in a play, donning different outfits for an infinite number of roles, and the universe is a stage—but what's behind that dark curtain?

"You sure are stormy tonight, Terra," he says, preferring to call Earth by its "female" name, Terra, which he says in all the interviews. "You're a tumultuous lady, aren't you?" He doesn't raise his voice over wave roar; he lets his words get drowned and lost in sea gargle. "You've never offered me hospitality, yet you're fighting hard to keep me here, using lightning swords to battle my spaceship."

Another vision wafts into his thoughts: warm apple dumplings, glazed carrots, homemade rolls, hot chocolate with marshmallows. Camped out in a chimney-ed cabin as cozy as a lakeside lodge. Comfy pajamas, comfy socks, comfy couch, snowy windows, Christmas lights, a fireplace crackling like static from a vintage Victrola. Flames from royal-blue candles illuminating the brass of the menorah on the hearth's mantel. No doubt a vision created by his hungry stomach, sore throat, achy cold body, and fondness of the holidays; as a boy, he celebrated both Christmas and Hanukkah.

"Fried chocolate doughnuts from that charming little Chocolate Truffle Inn sure would be comforting on this cold wet night," he says to no one, as coughs come out between his words. Every time the astronaut comes back to Earth after a space mission, he stays at Chocolate Truffle Inn, orders room service, hangs the "do not disturb" sign on his door for a week, and goes off for long periods to swim or kayak or hike, depending on the season. "Are there any aliens out there who own bed and breakfasts for tired star travelers?"

The sailor's jet ski arrives at the wedded husband rock. As he turns off the engine, the sky lightly *weeps* on him. At least the sky appears to be crying to those with poetic predispositions or a penchant for pantheism (the belief that *one* soul comprises everything) or an affinity for animism (the belief that *all* things, living and non, have a unique, individual spirit), thus to the pantheist and animist and poet, the sky can weep because it has a soul, just like the married rocks. More of those looney, sentimental, childhood thoughts about matchmaker gods and souls and destined marriages.

The seaman dismounts his watercraft.

"Warm glazed yams would hit the spot too," he says, continuing his conversation with no one. He'll soon be trillions of miles away from anyone to talk to and from sweet potato pie too, unless this other world has evolved potatoes and inhabitants who know potatoes + nutmeg + brown sugar = good eats. Maybe he'll be the one who brings them that recipe, and they'll share an exotic, tasty new dish with him like the Aztecs introducing Europeans to chocolate.

Since the diver's breathing apparatus is detached from his mouth, his warm breath meets chilly air and becomes cold puffs of mist. Each breath is like sand dropping in an hourglass, taking the sailor nearer to Away from Here.

Don't leave yet, he hears in his thoughts. Just his imagination surely, or else he's turning bonkers, hearing voices.

Both rocks have nooks and crevices for climbing. With aching joints, he climbs the slippery, married stone, while trying to keep rubber flippers, stuck under his dive belt, from slipping out. Earth's inhospitable waves assault his wetsuit and grab at his BCD durable vest, fashioned like a lifejacket, for establishing buoyancy and storing gear. The uncaring ocean does not coddle him because of his cold; saltwater continues lashing him.

"Thanks for the parting gift," he says to the mean old sea.

The same rude waves threaten to destroy his bobbing jet ski…and that special blue orb, he senses.

Enough of that baloney.

"Happy Holidays," he says to the husband rock and pats it like a pal.

He sits on the rock and slips on the flippers, while enduring the painfully cold and windy night with a stoicism usually only attained by a rock. His stony face gets hit by drizzle, as he gazes heavenward toward his future…*home*? His view is muddled by tears from the crying sky; the teardrops break across his goggles.

Mars, the rose of the celestial garden, is in full bloom, shining red. But out there, in the wilds, what wildflower worlds grow?

Wondering what's *out there*, the astronaut stands on the monolith with one hand (the flashlight-topped hand) firm on the hip of his leg pushed forward, the other hand suspended by his stationary leg, as if only half of the journeyer is eager, ready to go (to find *her*?), the other half reluctant, wanting to stay here (to find *her*?), but maybe only a poet would read the wanderer's stance that way.

From a nylon vest pocket, the star sailor takes out his old-fashioned compass, brass like the instruments of an ancient sailing vessel. The public thinks that the brass chain, often seen in photos dangling from his belt loop to his pocket, is the chain of a pocket watch. But no. If he had a special gal, she might probe him with questions about the interesting compass: How long have you had it? Where'd you get it? What does it mean to you? Questions she'd use to find out who he is, during the exploratory phase of the intense journey to Coupledome, questions she'd use to figure out what to get him for the holidays. Instead of being explored by her soft curious hands on this Christmastime night, the compass gets slugged by ill-natured waves, slugging the compass's arrow out of place.

He feels worried…about…the Neptune-blue orb with red river and…

Stop that nonsense!

He slips the compass back into vest pocket.

Slowly drifting from somewhere is *The Mermaid's Song*. Sounds like Joe "Cinnamon" Blugey on the horn. Who's the singer? Jo Stafford? Glenda Goodall? Not quite their voices. A siren's song?

Come, and I will lead the way
Where the pearly treasures be

The astronaut looks around. Is he being watched? He turns on the flashlight and studies the shadowy beach with 1200 investigating lumens beaming out from atop his closed hand.

Isolated in winter, the abandoned black-sand beach looks as dark as charcoal. Cold, unlit. Not even a glint of crystalline minerals. Mushy from drizzle. Like a charcoal grill left in the rain. The investigating flashlight reveals there's not even a crumb of jollity leftover from campfires on the barren beach. No roasted marshmallows. No thermoses of hot cocoa. No campfires at all. No ghost of warmth. The gloomsome landscape is a long way from *the* bon voyage party, where media and spectators have amassed on bleachers, balconies, boats, around jumbotrons and campfires, with binoculars and telephoto cameras and any device that offers spy-close views, to watch *an* astronaut leave Earth. But the history-making scene is not too crowded because most would rather be at home with their families during the holidays. Plus, it's raining. Even so, the whole world will view an astronaut's exit from Earth, thanks to TV and all other forms of surveillance that cannot stare beyond the surface. A celebrated sendoff the space voyager will receive.

Will *she* be watching from here or elsewhere, somewhere capable of picking up Earth's TV signals?

All those other spectators don't care that his throat hurts. Not those strangers who are always coming up to an astronaut, patting his shoulder, calling him by his last name, as if he's pals with a world that doesn't even know his favorite song.

Come with me, and we will go

Flash-light appears like a spaceship descending to Earth, creating a circle of light over black sand with its lit-up saucer underbelly. Up and down the astronaut moves his wrist and the attached flashlight, making the "spaceship" land on the beach then quickly ascend, land then quickly ascend.

His hours on Earth slowly dissipate…

"Maybe Santa Claus is an alien," he says, "and his sleigh is actually a spaceship."

How would the press describe his current behavior? "Strange"?

The explorer's flashlight keeps searching the beach for snoopers, but the light can only peer so far. Paparazzi have telephoto lenses that can spy details of a teeny tiny bikini on a teeny tiny woman on a teeny tiny sailboat a hundred miles off the coast, trying to make out if the woman is an actress, model…

Those snoopers never care that the astronaut has spent more time developing his brain muscle than his chest muscles, a lot of time reading in quietness; Top Gun or not, as an undergrad, most of his hours went by in Goldell University's stain-glassed Carl Edward Library, one of his classmates reported on a gossip website (the same classmate that disclosed the astronaut was an oddball in school, who had social allergies and never belonged to cliques, and this classmate found it "ludicrous" that the shy nerdy astronaut was a playboy and not a virgin with a distain for flirting, bars, and other manly hangouts). That's unlike his father, Jessie, the masculine sex symbol actor, who was always sociable, sporty, shirtless, and hard-chested on the beach, spiking volleyballs, for the world to savor. Jessie, a combination of macho and prissy like a gun in a rhinestone holster, was a stuntman in the 70s and 80s before he became a minor star. Jessie said about his son to a magazine, "Maybe he'll lose that paunch in space since there are no French Fry Huts and snack machines out there."

Merriment from a carnival on the faraway pier doesn't drown *The Mermaid's Song*. The merriment, as raucous as the waves, can be heard from miles around like distant fireworks, which will blast through dawn but never land on this dark charcoal and light it up.

Come with me, and we will go
Where the rocks of coral grow

Where is that song coming from?

The space explorer continues to eye search the desolate dark landscape, while creating paths of light across charcoal rocks with the flashlight. Light crawls up a boulder and looks from side to side: the only footprints in the gravelly soil are his own, leading out to the shoreline from a small cave, where he changed into scuba gear earlier. In the backdrop are black mountains that appear made of wet ink, dabbed here and there with highlights of silvery sharp edges. This dreary painting of a lonesome wet beach scene, not too Christmas-y, also includes shadows of wine country vineyards and silhouetted stucco mansions, including his own, hovering tall and gravely like headstones on gothic Poe-ish crags.

Another vision: the midnight-blue cloak is wrapped around a peculiar little figure (like a hunched little Yoda?), and the Neptune-blue orb is clasped by a little…*mitt?*...the color of Jupiter. The strange, Jupiter-colored creature, walking with an odd cane (?), is on a mission. The astronaut wants to protect it; in his old-timey heart, he feels that sad old tune *Someone to Watch Over Me.*

Follow, follow, follow me

His thoughts are really getting far out! Soon, he'll start thinking he's a Jedi whose destiny is to battle Darth Vader on The Death Star, or he's Frodo on a journey to destroy the One Ring of Power!

In the shadowy distance, a rocky precipice is lined on one side by a dark highway and gated on the other side by chain link fence. His sports car sits alone and looks like a sinuous creamy morsel of brown caramel. The fence's gate is closed because he closed it soon after opening it then made his way down to the beach with his scuba gear.

Surely the mysterious figure he sees up there by the fence is just a bush, not some shy cloaked soul, crouched down and loving him from afar, wishing to ask him, not *an* astronaut, but him, to stay on Earth…or to come with her to her world? Is she yearning to make him some warm holiday soup, made with a Planet X recipe with Planet X spices and herbs, to soothe his cold? But afraid of being spotted by an unmutual feeling of love, she stays safe behind the fence? No, most likely it's just a bush. Or that peculiar little figure in the damp cloak from his vision?

Satisfied—or disappointed?—that he has no one watching over him, the astronaut looks across the violent ocean to Launchpad 1, where crewwomen and crewmen continue working on noisy final preparations of history-making. Most of them are ready to take some much-earned time off for the holidays to be with their families.

"Two passengers will be aboard," the astronaut said at a press conference, "yours truly and human *hope* for deeper cosmic exploration. There will be a stowaway onboard too: humanity's *fear* of deeper cosmic exploration."

He shines his light one more time across the precipice, but the mysterious figure is gone. So, it wasn't a bush, unless bushes have learned to walk. Probably some west coast bobcat, or sneaky paparazzi. Surely not "a special gal, blowing him a farewell kiss."

He turns back to the malicious sea and uses the flashlight to make Morse Code—"Danger, Will Robinson, Danger!" Behavior that would definitely be labeled "strange." But no one on Launchpad 1 gets the faint light's *Lost in Space* signal. He tries another hokey message—"I need vegetable soup, stat, or peppermint hot cocoa." No one gets that message either, and even if they do, they're too busy to bother with juvenile messages.

"Why is it," the explorer asks of the stars, "that when an astronaut dedicates his life to finding a friend in space, he's considered heroic, but when a grown man on Earth dedicates his life to the same discovery, he's labeled pathetic?"

The reticent stars look awfully frosty.

The pioneer of spaceflight returns his gaze to the antagonistic ocean, where the long-standing married rocks are the picture of stability. To the peaceful husband, he says, "Want to switch places with me? You go up there and I stay here." Wind and rain bat his words like a baseball. "How 'bout it, rock? You want to go instead? No? I can see why." The starfarer blows a kiss to the why then says to the wife rock, "Ah, too shy to send a kiss back to me, or too loyally in love with your husband? For the best. Because I have to leave, soon, the sooner the better, and you'll never see me again, darling. Why would I stay on a world that doesn't respond to my Morse Code? Terra never wanted to marry me. No, the Earth never has been my wife, offering a home."

Yes, come, behold what treasures lie

Only after a leap that leads to another world, the explorer enters the uninviting ocean. His arrival is greeted with tossing waves that seem intent on launching him out, yet contradictorily, a heavy force seems intent on swallowing the sailor into the unknown. He doesn't fight against the monstrous sea, "the sea beast," but instead allows his being to get used to the roughness, to the coldness, to "tough it out" and fin a path for himself to follow: to the monolith's foundation.

Undoubtedly, diving alone is not safe, especially when one is suffering a cold on a stormy night, but this is an individual willing to be hurled into the deep bays of outer space, alone, knowing no one on Earth has a long enough rope to reach out to him if things go wrong. No SOS can be responded to at that distance.

However, the still sea of space won't be so rough, will it? Who knows for sure about those deep recesses.

Away far below the rolling waves—how is that song able to penetrate thick waves?

Vast murky water. Pinpoints of moonlight appear as stars. Swirls of water glow like nebulae in flashlight haze. The astronaut looks as if he's snorkeling through the mysterious universe. A late-night dolphin passes by like a mini submarine.

Even though the water is cold, it's nothing like Antarctica, where the mariner has gone diving and kayaking amongst icebergs, where it felt like being inside a refrigerator's freezer, but the explorer got to watch humpback whales, and swim with penguins and sea butterflies, and voyage the otherworldly aqua-hued ice that made him feel like he was journeying Pluto.

A soothing ocean lullaby and the sea meadow are lovely, but the sailor can't be lured into a false sense of serenity by the beauty, because a sharp-toothed eel could be lurking in the seagrass.

Sea flowers, bouquets of them, the astronaut paddles by.

Overt riches, hid from human eye,

Unflinchingly, his eyes are viewing nautical Earthlings somewhat up close.

Like organ pipes, coral rise up and are as colorful as crayons.

Most of the mariner's human skin, aside from his tan manicured hands and ankles the color of toffee, is covered in slick rubber and nylon. Do any of the ocean creatures see him as one of them?

Nope, they don't accept him as sea life—he's the alien here, frightening, to be avoided. None get too close to the foreigner who doesn't belong here with his phony flippers, mask, and air tank that were purchased in a store, not naturally selected. These seafarers are all searching for food, safety, shelter, while bonehead human is searching for… what? Well, not a one of them gets him either, and the astronaut keeps swimming his lone path, fighting against the beast of a sea.

At least no crab claws at his wallet. No reefs brush against him to have fame rub off on them. You're not famous in our world, jack, and your VIP status doesn't grant you entrances into our clubs, and our sharks can't be bought off with cash.

The water feels softer, or maybe it's his imagination, but as the explorer dives deeper, the water feels easier, "swimmed in" like a walkpath that has been smoothed by a previous voyager.

Extraordinarily, years ago, when he was a child diving in this section of the ocean, he saw a being that looked like some glorious extraterrestrial mermaid. Vacationing on Earth? Stranded on Earth? Or an unidentified Earthling species? Whoever, whatever she was, what if she was swimming here again?

The floodlight tries to penetrate murkiness.

On that holiday afternoon in childhood, the aqua sea was lit by shafts of sunlight, where schools of tropically colored fish swam through a kelp forest as golden as wheat. After he spotted her and her graceful swimming, swimming as professionally as any dolphin or turtle, she hid behind mossy stone, where she coyly peeked to watch him too. The stone beside her made her look like a soft creature poking out from a round seashell. She seemed too delicate for the sea but so do guppies. Almost flirtatiously, her long, flowing, *hair* (?) swayed and bobbed behind her, a trail of shimmering silky pink like a unicorn's mane. Like a rainbow coalesced to form phantastic *her*. She probably wasn't a mermaid, at least not of the Earthly variety; but she did have a humanoid shape and a short, phosphorescent fin, glowing greenish blue like the aurora borealis of the sea. Small, nymph-ish, and young perhaps, she wore, on the top half of her figure, what looked like some sort of spacesuit, also green and shiny in color but material-like, not flesh-like, and the suit covered her hands (?) shaped like mitts. It wasn't a spacesuit exactly but maybe a diving suit, like she was adapted to the seas of another world but had to use specialized equipment to swim in Earth's seas. Her pink hair was free, not contained in helmet. But her face…her face…her extraordinary face was at the end of a tunnel of light in the aqua water…her face was somewhat revealed in the helmet's window that reflected sunlight every which way like a child's drawing of the sunball with sunbeams…well, the explorer had never seen a face like that: alien big eyes like a Grey from Roswell, no nose, lips (if she had lips) concealed by sunlight and edge of helmet. The two youngsters played a game of "hide-n-seek" in the sea forest, as she hid behind kelp and swam deeper and deeper until the waters turned from honey tea to soda pop blue to dark coffee, and he shyly followed, not knowing if she wanted him to follow her or if she was trying to escape him. She was as precious and fantastic as a seahorse or starfish. In the thirty-one years that have passed since that moment, never has his secret heart beat so hard, not even when he saw Mars approaching through his ship's porthole.

Over the years, he kept their meeting a secret. He never told anyone of his discovery because he was afraid people would hunt for her like *The Creature from the Black Lagoon.* Many people claim they want to find exotic life on another world, yet they despise exotic life on their own world, where differences are shunned, ridiculed, and hated.

Well, if he is being truthful with himself, how many times has he dived, hoping to find her swimming here again? How many times has he traveled in space, wishing to see her "swimming" amongst the stars, wishing to "bump" into her by fate on the shores of another planet?

Every which way, he continues looking around the algae-green water.

And what if she has held onto feelings for him all these years? He has held onto feelings for her (if he is being honest with himself), unspoken feelings, feelings of love and kinship that somehow traveled across the sea to one another's fledgling hearts. What if she was the unidentified creature he saw upon the beach precipice? Maybe she has grown up and was enjoying a moment on land and watching him from afar before he departs Earth?

Lithely, a vision swims into his thoughts: again, of the little, cloaked, Yoda-ish figure and the blue orb with red equator. How is that figure and the orb connected to *her*?

Later, after his extraordinary encounter, after chalking the experience up to a delusion, the astronaut told that story from his childhood about seeing the sea creature, in one of his first scientific articles about the unlikeliness of UFOs visiting Earth ("Humans just aren't that interesting to attract visitors"). He never confessed the story was from his *own* childhood. He never mentioned which sea, just in case she was real and he still did not want anyone to hunt for her. Instead, he wrote that he had used the "fictitious" tale as an example of "strange sightings." He also did not mention his other childhood experiences of seeing peculiar lights in the sky, etc. He claimed "the science-fiction-crazed kid" had only seen what the kid had hoped to see: "some sort of alien mermaid adolescent adapted to the ocean of another world." But an intuitive reader should have sensed the truth: the story was from his own life. But even his mother hadn't sensed it. Instead, she had trapped the article in a pretty picture frame in her mansion and stuck it on the wall to be admired, not read.

Dimly shine in
ocean's caves

The underwater light reveals that at his base, the husband rock is also oddly shaped like his wife. This is where the "Martian" mermaid had bashfully swum away until she plunged into the virgin depths and was lost from his sight—what if the depths lead into a singularity, right into another world, her world, or the galaxy's core, or beyond?

Ha, more of those nutty thoughts!

Astronaut rubs his immaculate hand against dingy ancient stone; this is what the explorer does: reaches out to exotic worlds.

Nautical rope, as thick as ship rope, is tied around the monolith's base.

Keenly, another vision jolts the mariner like a lightning bolt zapped through the sea: the Neptune-blue orb—*she* wore that on her spacesuit/diving suit! Encased in a halter, the orb shined right in the center of her flat chest, shimmered right through the water separating them in childhood, and the light was a sight as beautiful as bare breasts to his young eyes. Remembering that moment is like uncovering sunken treasure. Her fingerprints are on so many of his treasured memories, aren't they, even memories she does not physically star in, reminiscences like sitting on the married rock on a bright afternoon, his bare toes in water rolling with sunlight, and hoping to see *her* splash up from the sea like a friendly dolphin.

Good gracious, jolted by the memory, the explorer can barely strengthen the knot around the husband rock. The location of the tatty rope's other end is unseen in cloudy waters but it's easy to intuit where it leads. The underwater lantern scans the rope's twines, searching for any tears, as the Milky Way mariner continues his journey toward the rope's other end on this secret voyage in the frigid sea.

On reaching the rope's other end, wrapped like a wedding ring around the wife rock, the explorer tightens that knot too, not such an historical event—tightening the bond between some old married rocks. Maybe this world is not suitable for *him* either—greed, lust, fear, and ego have never made many of his decisions. Most of his choices are decided by his inner sense of rightness, his Boy Scout duty to honor and courage, his compassion for all life, and his old-fashioned heart's romanticism as sentimental as the holidays. That brand of good-guy hero went out with Flash Gordon, so chides his publicist mother, who tries to keep that "hokey" side of her son out of the press, where it would be laughed to pieces. Tightening the rocks' bond, he is like Old Man Heng in the legend of Old Man Heng and Old Lady Meng, two mythical beings who work in conjunction with the lunar matchmaker. Heng and Meng are also responsible for bringing soulmates together in each lifetime, in each reincarnation, in a twofold process: one) by concocting a "potion" that makes the lovers forget their former lives in their new incarnations, and two) by allowing them to retain a vague memory of their past lives, their forever love: a longing for one another, a tug on the red thread of fate, a tug known as yearning. Both the forgetting and the remembering make the eternal hide-n-seek game so pleasurable.

Dear heavens, the opening above the core of the rock looks like a heart, at least to a poet. The explorer switches the flashlight from wide beam to focused beam to get a more detailed view. Did *she* ever see this—this heart inside a stone?

He rubs his hand around the rock's hidden heart, delicately, as if stone can break.

Lodged inside the rock's heart shape is a dented Biskatine Cocoa tin, "Special Christmas recipe with peppermint," says the faded label, decorated in one of those 1920's-esque cherub-looking drawings of a rosy-cheeked boy and a rosier-cheeked girl, clad in winter coats and earmuffs and taking a break from building a snowman to share a cup of cocoa at Christmastime. Just junk? That got swept in by a wave?

The astronaut looks around the tumultuous ocean and sees only hazy water full of unknowns.

Surely not just junk—the cocoa tin is too perfectly, purposely?, placed inside the rock's opening. The heart's point is positioned right atop the center of the tin's lid, creating two exact sides of the heart, the girl in the drawing in one side, the boy in the other.

What if *she*, the playful mermaid, planted the cocoa tin in the rock's heart for him to find like a holiday gift?

The astronaut reaches out for the cylindrical cocoa tin like an archeologist from a movie who has unearthed a rare magical artifact.

The explorer doesn't need any special diving suit for this exploration, just curiosity. Free of tank and gear and cradled by the soft bosom of the mossy matrimonial rock, he sits long legs dangling with the cocoa tin in his lap like a child putting together a new toy at Christmas. Foamy, salted water thrashes his bare toes, but he ignores the flogging from the sea beast. The wind's loud and damp, freezing, the rubber suit's bunchy, his body shivers, he's achy sick, and his face is wet, more from drizzle than sea, but he doesn't have time to mess with any of that—finding out what's inside the holiday tin is too interesting to waste time away from it. After all, the astronaut's an explorer who seeks interestingness hidden in unknowns, or not so hidden, just unexplored.

He surely wishes he had some Kissling chocolates or Fudgy Mounds or anything chocolate to munch on for his last holiday ever spent on Earth. Instead, he clears his throat, swallows phlegm, and wipes his runny nose with the edge of his index finger. He doesn't remove the neoprene diving hood, which keeps his hair and sideburns out of his way; they get enough exposure from the media. ("His black hair shines because the shampoo he uses makes his dark locks as luxurious as expensive fabric," wrote a reporter, instead of writing about singularities.)

While the world continues to celebrate his upcoming departure, he looks around, making sure he's not being watched, but he can't see much through fog. He's careful not to look in the area where he saw the shadowy figure on the precipice (the otherworldly mermaid on shore?). This time he seems genuinely satisfied that he's not being observed; mist is doing a fine job of making the world beyond the married rock disappear and making the astronaut disappear from the world's view.

"I'm getting that found-a-message-in-a-bottle kind of feeling!" the radio astronomer, who uses his life to search for signals from space, says to the wife, his voice revealing more than it does at press conferences.

Roars from the ocean waves are drowned by the waves pounding in his ears from the big beats of his excited boyhood heart.

Now he hears that old Christmas tune, *It Came Upon the Midnight Clear.*

Oh, rest beside the weary road
And hear the angels sing!

He slips his dry ear out from the neoprene cap, holds the wet container beside his bare ear, and gently rattles the cocoa tin's contents. Something's inside. Not too heavy but not as light as cocoa powder either.

The blue orb?

The scientist likes to imagine what could be, but in a moment like this, patience can't win against curiosity, so he tenderly pops off a tightly sealed aluminum lid. A genie doesn't billow up, but a strong scent of chocolate does like the wafting from a warm pot of hot cocoa. No water gushes out. The contents aren't water damaged. But it's too dark and misty to make out what those contents are. Now, time to reach inside. A trace of trepidation on his face, a face that usually doesn't reveal any of his emotions.

"A venomous sea creature might be in here and electrocute me with a tentacle of death," he says to the rock. "In an old sci-fi B-movie maybe. On this world, there might be some drugs in here, stolen money, a sex toy, who knows. Hopefully not." Then he confesses the true cause of his trepidation, "That would be disappointing."

But a scientist cannot be scared of disappointment, and an astronaut cannot be scared of any creature he might encounter *out there*, or at least, he cannot let fear stop him from finding such a creature or from finding nothing at all.

Oh, hush the noise, ye men of strife,
And hear the angels sing!

Slowly tilting the tin, the explorer holds out his bare palm under the tin's opening, since it's more respectable to allow the contents to come to him instead of forcing them out. The container's goods slide against metal until out drops…

A handheld transistor radio.

The radio rests in the region of the explorer's hand bordered by what palmists call "the fate line" and "the heart line" (his boyhood home was populated with New Age-y Hollywood types interested in things like palmistry and astrology).

The astronaut looks into the now empty tin and sees his own moonlit reflection at the end of the tunnel.

The Christmas carol slowly fades away into the mist, and ocean slosh is what he hears.

The cosmic mariner turns his attention back to the bounty. The small rectangular radio is vintage, small enough to fit in a breast pocket. The radio has the mahogany color of antique furniture. It's a pretty little piece of machinery. Against the lines of his thumb, he feels the speaker that looks like some old heating grate. Above the speaker, an on/off switch is at the top left. Beside the switch is a dial changer, a golden circle about the size of a silver dollar with jagged edges like a coin meant to be rotated by the thumb to change stations.

An old radio? Inside an old dented cocoa tin? Hidden in the base of an old sea rock? Junk tossed away by a teenager in the 1920s or 1950s? Or *her* holiday gift to the star sailor?

Before the scientist conjectures, his fingertips detect slightly elevated rough spots scattered across the back of the smooth radio like breadcrumbs along flat surface. He turns the music machine around and sees what looks like half-inch-tall "hieroglyphics" painted in Neptune-blue, spelling out a phrase in the exotic written language.

"It can't be!" the astronaut says like a skeptic who has died and gone to a Heaven he never believed in, where his surprise quickly dissipates into joy, big holiday-ish JOY! "I'm the only one who knows this language—I'm the only one who knows it because *I'm* the one who made it up!"

The alientologist reads the message, written in the strange language, again and again, as if he reads it enough times, he'll be forced to believe what he is seeing.

"I spent my childhood making up those hieroglyph-type symbols," he says, continuing his candid conversation with the wife rock. "My own secret language. Yet,"—his press-conference voice breaking across the rock and his childhood voice gushing out—"here it is written on this radio, in my own secret language, 'Herein contains a message to be deciphered by Captain Elvin.'"

The explorer's face looks like that of a sage who has encountered a glorious riddle.

Suddenly, skepticism clouds his briefly radiating face.

"You weren't my radio, were you?" Disappointment comes out undisguised from his voice, alone in the fog. "Some old 'message in a bottle' I made myself, years ago, a message to future me, using my made-up moniker, Captain Elvin. I was always doing things like that. Plus, I collected vintage cocoa tins, those fabulous old canisters from Kissling Cocoa and Biskatine and Hershey's."

He thinks about it, doesn't discover an answer in his memories of growing up close to this "charcoaled" shoreline.

"Well, I certainly don't remember you," he says to the radio that is getting tiptapped by rain sprinkles, just like his diving cap.

He pulls out the little, slim, golden antenna from the radio's top. He doesn't change the dial. Most likely, the radio's set on the frequency it needs to be for transmitting the "message to be deciphered by Captain Elvin." He flips the on switch. Surprisingly, the old battery-operated radio comes to life, radiating The Beatles' *Dear Prudence.* Strangely, there is no static, no garble of any sort.

The astronomer looks around, searching for a radio tower out there, somewhere, in mist transmitting this music, but all he sees are flirtatious stars peeking in and out of fog.

In this moment, the radio astronomer is more interested in deciphering the message from the little transistor radio than in understanding the radio waves in the Milky Way's core.

The radio only sings a snippet of *Dear Prudence* before beaming *Star Tripper.* Again, only a portion of the song is played. After twenty minutes, numerous snippets of different songs have leaked out from the mysterious radio. Then there's silence. No static, just silence. Who is broadcasting this? This "message to be deciphered by Captain Elvin." Suddenly, *Dear Prudence* starts up again, the same snippet, then Harry Chapin's *Star Tripper* again…

"Doesn't it figure—right when I'm about to leave Earth, I find something captivating like this that makes me want to stick around for a while?"

~~~~~

Now two sets of footprints lead to and fro the beach cave, both his own.

Along his barefoot walk in cold dark sand, his eyes searched for other footprints, wondering if the mermaid had walked on this wet desolate beach. Maybe she can shed her fin on land and gain legs. But either she had not wandered this beach, or wind or waves or drizzle had swept away her footprints, or maybe the otherworldly creature didn't leave "footprints."

His own bare soles are getting poked by hard earth.

The explorer's wet, clunky, diving gear rests against a gritty cave wall, a long rest, unless someone finds the gear, because the astronaut will not be diving again on this planet, at least not beneath water. Whoever can keep the jet ski too.

The grim cave, that looks carved out of a piece of charcoal, offers as much comfort and hospitality as a hospital bathroom. Heavy fog acts like a curtain over the craggy opening, as the explorer dries himself with
~~~~~

towel. His bodily self is nude except for wearing a twine necklace, where a small chunk of raw diamond hangs down in a thicket of black chest hair. His nude self smells slightly like oatmeal and honey.

The astronaut's well-kempt dry clothes, designer shoes, and shiny wallet—his suit and gear for making his way in this world—are laid out on a boulder beside his compass and holiday gifts: cocoa tin and excavated radio whose golden antenna has been slipped back inside. But where's his phone?

The inhospitable night keeps getting colder, windier, louder, and stormier; his nose keeps dripping and a cough shakes his chest roughly like a hurricane battering a ship. This is what he gets for rejecting a time in quarantine before his voyage. His throat is getting more swollen. A sip of hot cocoa from Chocolate Truffle Inn would feel like a snuggle against grandma. Nothing sounds more appealing than lying his aching body in a soft bed and pulling the covers up over himself and *her*, if a mermaid can snuggle with a man in bed, and taking a nap together until they're rested enough for in-depth lovemaking. He'd like a hot shower too, with *her*, but no showering for three hours after a dive, or else risk decompression sickness.

Another vision: the little cloaked creature, with odd cane and Neptune orb in pouch, walking up a winding dark stairwell, amongst the stars and fog. Is all that somehow connected with the strange radio?

That's just fine and dandy—he's going to go bonkers right before his mission, and the whole darn world is counting on him.

The latch over the door of his emotions has been lifted, the door that often gets locked in adulthood to keep embarrassing feelings from sprinting free and bumping painfully against ridicule; the lock over *that* door has been lifted, or rather *yanked* open by the force of the exciting discovery of the mysterious radio. A few boyish smiles run out from hiding, as the astronaut covers the rest of himself and his natural scent with clothes, and he eventually barricades the hopeful smiles with Doubt.

An igloo-white flight jacket, pinned with gold wings that showcase his status as astronaut (the kind of cool jacket a kid dreams of wearing someday), adds a touch of futuristic spacecar-racer hotshot to an outfit otherwise suitable for a morning at a 1940s library: collared shirt the color of marble cake with marbled buttons, cable-knit sweater vest reminiscent of maple syrup, and chocolate-brown pants with matching wingtip shoes. The corduroy pants reveal nothing of the masculine landscape, unlike some men who show off the "hills." His own mother says he should show off more. For the fans. Considering the star's elite status, one might expect his clothes to smell like a men's magazine full of expensive cologne ads, but instead his clothing has no smell other than fabric, no scent to announce his entering or exiting anywhere; his famous face does enough of that.

The cosmic mariner attaches the old-fashioned compass to his belt loop, as if he is a runaway child who needs direction. The compass's slim brass chain, as knotty as chains that anchor ships, dangles down into the star sailor's right pocket, and the compass's range reaches all the way to the planet's core.

Now time to explore his last Earthly discovery...

~~~~~

The astronaut drives his vintage brown sports car with one hand on the wheel, a confidence with machines developed from years of piloting and hot-rodding. He eats a Biskatine Chocolate Bar in between sneezes and coughs. Singing along to Jackson Browne, he cruises at 75 miles per hour on coastal highway, but his heart beats much faster, thinking of the radio's message and the orb and *her*, just like a kid at the holidays, imagining his presents.

The winetown beach looks like an ink sketch of the lonesome sea at night, and *Late for the Sky* is a fitting song for the rainy scene. The "nerd's" "sexy" car, all caramel-colored muscles designed to go a lot faster than this, drives far beyond his five-car garage, private airplane hangar, two private cabin cruisers Cosmic Mariner and Mer-Explorer, and for-sale modern beach house that is shaped more like a figure from a geometry textbook than a home, filled with almost every-*thing* he has, all boxed up and waiting to be sold, and the home's impenetrable gates are suitable for Alcatraz.

"I despise wine, yet I live in wine town," he says to the radio, who rides in the passenger seat, better than talking to no one. "Jessie's always downing fine vintages from Cosimo Vineyard. Ah, good ol' dad—he drinks bourbon like it's testosterone. Like father, not like son."

Far in the distance above the beach pier, fireworks spell out "Goodbye!" But as mist coats the car's windows, the farewell message disappears
~~~~~

from the astronaut's view. Now here the explorer is alone in the darkness of Earth night, voyaging this planet for the last time in a small, wheeled ship with a mahogany dashboard of instrument panels.

He senses *her* nearness. Doesn't he? Or is he nuts?

No more time to squander, the message needs probing. The roadship's caramel coating becomes ironic—caramel pours *slowly*—as the car zooms up to 140, thanks to the astronaut's wingtip shoe commanding the accelerator, just like a boy, playing spaceship.

The car's freezing interior doesn't smell like caramel but like old car-seating fabric and a trace of chocolate. The steering wheel is smudged in chocolate fingerprints, since the driver often holds candy bars bare without the wrapper while also holding the ship's wheel. Sitting in the backseat is a Mars-red suitcase. Hanging around the rearview are a Robot toy and the astronaut's ID lanyard. The elite lanyard grants the rocketeer access to the launchpad and pretty much anywhere else he wants to go, even into women's bedrooms, but what about *her* bedroom—would his hotshot ID open that up for him too? "Hopefully not," he says aloud, to no one. Riding in the passenger seat beside the strange radio are the excavated cocoa tin, a Groucho Marx disguise, and a canvas tote bag, no less conversationalists than the celebrity's usual passengers—bureaucrats and bimbos. One such passenger once asked, "What's that strange device hanging from the rearview?" He said, "That's B9." She responded, "I didn't realize it was something for the space program." She had never heard of *Lost in Space*! So, he explained, "It's a toy model of the robot from the iconic TV show." "Oh," she said, and her cackle stabbed—"How silly."

"I guess I'm already trillions of miles away from anyone to talk to, eh?" he says to the radio. "I better hope for a planet with a stream to swim in and tall mountain to climb—things I can enjoy by *myself*, since I will be by all by myself, unless…"

Before heading to space, the astronaut made a stop at an Earth landmark: the grocery store, Greeda's. His cheesy Groucho disguise, always stored in the glove compartment, hadn't fooled anyone into believing that's what he looked like, but it garnered the unrecognizable star enough precious time to get a few goodies without being stopped—no one wanted to approach "the crazy person" in self-checkout. Besides, the world's most famous playboy wouldn't be spending his last night on

Earth buying brownies, would he? He also bought a bottle of ease-a-cold medicine syrup. Afterwards, "the crazy person" gave all the cash in his wallet to a homeless man, named Tag, outside in the unfriendly cold with his friendly dog. In fact, the astronaut gave Tag his entire wallet, after taking a few things out of the moneycoddler like a key; Mars doesn't take cash or American Express, at least not yet, and the generous gene Z undoubtedly thrives in cashless environs. The astronaut petted the pug's head and said, "I'm gonna miss your kind." Maybe some Earthlings, like dogs, do have the phantastic gene Z. He offered Tag, "May your holidays get brighter." Ironically, the *homeless* man said, "I hope you find your home," as if he was a mystic in disguise as a drifter—maybe the old lunar matchmaker?

The astronaut talks again to the radio, his only companion for the night, "I once read 'If you're only nice to *certain* people, you're not nice at all.' I learned that from a book by Sidereus Sterling, not from my folks. I learned morals from writers, songs, comic books, at least *good* morals. Jessie and Mother had their own kind of 'morals.' Like Mother's golden rule: 'Never die on the same day someone more famous than you dies—they'll get all the attention.'"

The approaching stony mountain, draped in green grass, stands like a big, tall, Christmas tree with pointed top, perfect for a star to perch on, and mist circles around the mountain like garland.

The expensive car's heater is broken! A fine how-do-you-do for ninety thousand dollars. So, the voyager's hands stay cold, turning metal-like because of the chill. Well, he needs to get used to cold, because the astronaut is soon to be frozen like a Popsicle to stay "fresh" on a long voyage through the coldest of coldness—infinite space.

"Colonel Cute" uses the back of his cold hand to wipe his drippy cold nose then wipes his hand down his corduroy pants—you won't see that photo in magazines. Heroes don't get colds, the public must assume. His publicist/mother once lectured, "A one-moment sneeze in public takes a lifetime to live down."

With cold fingers, he rolls the music dial to another station. The vintage car's sound system has modern upgrades but retains its old-fashioned visage, which looks right singing the classic *Dream a Little Dream of Me.* Sneezing, coughing, and chomping on the candy bar, he sings along now with Glenda Goodall, while rowdy thunder continues to be a loud, cursing drunk.

Lightning could become a skyblock to his voyage.

"Should I turn my phone on, hear updates about the mission?" he asks the radio. "No, I shouldn't? Well, sure, you'd think that, since you think I have something better to do with my last night on Earth, but this mission is very important, you know. Where even is my phone?" He looks around, pats a few pockets, still can't locate his phone. He pats his candy-bar-crafted paunch. "Mother said, 'We can work with pudge, makes you vulnerable, kind of cute.' Jessie no longer even goes out on his beloved beach, worried his aged body is no longer acceptable to be photographed."

Now the car's caramel color is no longer ironic, as the car flows *slowly*, not using its muscles but its skills to navigate a steep foggy mountain road which a writer might pen as a symbol for a less-traveled path to ascension. The winding "stairwell" around the mountain leads past grapevines and hubbub to the mountain's head (the coastal town's highest peak of solitude, above the fog).

The stairwell "to heaven" the little creature in his vision was walking?

Seemingly lightyears from the world's attention, an old planetarium and a separate observatory rest quietly on the summit of the grassy mountain, surrounded by damp green forest and a circle of fog that skirts the lower mountain. The explorer has arrived at Alone. The rounded, frost-white observatory has the shape of a snow globe with hollyberry-red base. The silver dome of the planetarium looks like a flying saucer landed on the roof of a brick and stone country house. No lights are on inside. Two four-paned windows on either side of the planetarium's door flash from lightning.

"The observatory was built not long after Griffith and Hayden, one of the oldest observatories around," the astronomer says, continuing his talk with the radio. "Now owned by yours truly."

The hotshot is smooth with his "landing" as the sports car slows to a stop in rain-slick grass.

Stepping into rain that touches so softly it could almost fool one into believing it is caring, the astronaut shuts the driver's door tenderly as if the car is a lady.

Thunder isn't tender, though, as it shatters nighttime quietness. The star's sneezes can't compete with the booming sky for loudest sound in the night, *quiet* sneezes, remember, his mother's adage. Well, his mother/publicist isn't here, neither are any press conference mics, so achoo achoo ACHOOOOOO! Beat that, thunder.

Looking at the glistening wet forest, all the shadows amongst the trees, hearing all the soft rustling in the brush, he feels *her* nearness like an animal sensing his mate is nearby.

Shivering and coughing, his body getting more swollen in a battle against cold, he puts the tote over his achy shoulder and lugs the red suitcase under the same arm.

Rain lands on his gold astronaut wings as he walks; the large chest of the golden bird showcases his rank as captain, bravest and mightiest of the flyers.

From his pocket, he takes an old-fashioned key for an old-fashioned lock, not a punch code or barcode or eye scanner. He opens the planetarium's front door, as wind throws rain onto him and tote bag, where the little radio peeks out.

From cold air to cold air. The electric fireplace is turned off.

With his icy reddened thumb, he flips the switch in the main room, where light comes from a chandelier made of faux candlesticks the color of old lace. He quickly shuts the door on brutal outside. Then locks it out.

Inside is a mix of earthy homey and sci-fi futurine. The rustic floor, gritty brick, tan and pale gray, is lighter than the walls, which are composed of darker stones embedded in gray mortar like a pilgrim's house.

The home smells dusty like a broom, or an old book, and that makes him cough more.

In a few glass display cases are artifacts from space and spaceflight history, standing as if in a museum: a Martian meteorite, the baseball he tossed on Phobos, a space capsule (in a large display case), Sidereus Sterling's typewriter, etc. On the cobbled walls are framed posters of space missions and sci-fi movies like *The Day Mars Invaded Earth* and Carl Sagan's *Cosmos* and Sterling's famous Treasure Map for otherworldly treasure. The chandelier's candlesticks also cast golden light across nautical artifacts, brass armillary globe and model ships, and baseball memorabilia like a signed pitcher's glove from Oscar Eddie Luna and a framed baseball jersey, Biskatine Bombers, from the Women's MLB. Also flickering in the candles' "flames" is an old flier for Zorman's Traveling Circus's sideshow: "Come see The Undead Girl! 10 cents!" Wouldn't the public think that was eccentric? On the right side of the doorway is a gumball dispenser shaped like a flying saucer (void of colorful gumballs). On the left side stands a life-size model of the silver robot from *The Outer Limits* episode "I, Robot"; the robot's round head is capped with a sailor's cap. The press would surely paint him as a loon if they ever glimpsed his private world. A few steps past the gumball dispenser, a square archway, that looks like a stone arch from a Middle Ages monastery, leads to a library nook, where the back wall is cobbly, and the two side walls are made of bookshelves, which have not been filled. Against the stone wall is a rustic table, where it's easy to imagine a monk reading scripture by candlelight, except for one peculiarity: a copper, diving helmet sitting on the table like decoration. A rolling ladder, for reaching books up high, stands still.

Almost everything is still, as if frozen in time, no movement of life to create the changes needed for time to be measured, such as how new carpet goes from plush to ragged from the movements of a family's feet.

Cold and shaky, the astronaut walks toward the counter, a tan semi-circular surface that resembles a *Star Trek* console, where customers once bought tickets to the light show. Yes, the public would definitely label a home that is part *Star Trek*, part medieval monastery, as weird.

He sets damp tote and red suitcase beside a replica of The Rosetta Stone and a small limestone statue of a mermaid with seashells over her breasts. The visitor counter has undergone a partial renovation into a kitchen, not as quaint as Chocolate Truffle Inn. A small, rose gold refrigerator is built underneath the counter. A brass sink shines like a brass porthole. A rectangular cutout in the counter is awaiting a stove, which would be much needed now for making warmth. To the left of the visitor counter is a door to a restroom, to the right, a door to the "universe."

Seeing that door feels like an electric current swam into his heart.

He takes off his wet nylon flight jacket and places it around the robot. The jacket took the brunt of most of the rain, which is running harder on the windows; the rain makes for good curtains and provides excellent music for creating dinner-for-one. With his sleeve cuff, he wipes rain mist off his face, eyebrows, and hair, while coughing.

Behind the counter, foot-long brass letters spell out "Sandra Horn Planetarium" beneath a train-station-style clock, ticking loudly on the stone wall; the large dark arrows of the "minute hand" and "hour hand" ominously circle through the astronaut's time left on Earth.

From the tote, he takes the bottle of medicine, pulls off the plastic safety strip, and takes a big swig of thick red liquid.

On the left, past the robot, a brick step leads about a foot down into a sitting room with a throw rug as soft and brown as gingerbread. A black electric fireplace is designed to look like a potbelly stove. The fireplace, ginger rug, and cobbly walls create cozy scenery for an old-timey Christmas. He flicks on the fireplace's side switch, but for some reason, the fireplace only makes an odd hum and doesn't blow out any warm air. He flicks it off. Excellent. More time in the cold. Why didn't he get the central heat repaired?

His pants are somewhat rain damp too, he now notices. So are his shoes. "Well, Happy Hanukkah to me, eh?" With his feet, he slips off the shoes and reveals brown socks decorated in little Jupiters.

One second, two seconds, closer to his future *home*? May not turn out to be a home at all.

In the bathroom, white pillar candles stand on deep recesses in the stone walls above the clawfoot tub, a romantic setting for making love to *her* for the first time, if alien mermaids can make love with humans. He turns on the sink, hoping to defrost his cold red fingers with hot water, but after letting the water run for two minutes and feeling it pour continuously as cold as the outdoor pipes, he turns off the brass knob. No hot water either! And where are the matches for lighting the candles? He sifts through drawers, finds nothing, no lighters, nothing for making warmth.

Back in the front room, he hears sleet hitting the roof and sees ice pellets making a frosty, bluish, "smoky" slush on the windows.

From the tote, he removes the curious radio and places her tenderly on the counter by Rosetta and limestone mermaid.

"I will figure you out," the astronomer says to the music radiator, while wiping raindrops from her antique frame with his fingertip. "I have a lifetime of practice in this area, just so you know, a boyhood spent fascinated with codebreaking, systems of numeration, hieroglyphics, cuneiform, Pig Latin..."

From the same tote, he removes a gallon drum of chocolate ice cream, all hard and frosted like it has spent time in cold stasis. He pulls off gold-colored lid and his icy fingertips get even redder in the process.

"I know it's not too smart to eat ice cream when I'm cold, but this will be my last chance to eat real chocolate ice cream. In fact, I plan to get so much of my fill of the stuff," he says, while dipping his finger into the ice cream and taking a big scoop, "I'll never want to eat it again, if that's possible." He licks ice cream from his fingertip. "Maybe not possible. One can never get his fill of heaven. But don't worry, I plan to balance the coldness. I won't freeze to death before deciphering your message."

Foraging the tote again, the explorer takes out a jar of hot fudge, old-fashioned and laced with a brown-checkered ribbon. "My hot date," he says, continuing his forthright talk with the peculiar radio. "There is no way I would squander my last night on Earth with a woman who has never seen *Lost in Space*."

The tote contains more treats: a half gallon of vegan coconut milk, and an aluminum pan of store-bought brownies, enclosed under a clear plastic lid with a red sale sticker on top ("Stansfield's Bakery, $3.99"), and a tin of Biskatine Cocoa.

"You might think I picked out Biskatine Cocoa because I found you in such a tin, but the reverse is actually true—Biskatine has always been my favorite, perfect combination of sugar and chocolate, and that's what drew my interest to your tin hideout."

In a depression in the wall is a small counter, where a mini microwaves sits, along with a cup rack for one lone mug, which he takes down.

"I wouldn't have agreed to this mission if I couldn't have cocoa in space. To quote Sterling, 'If you have never tasted hot chocolate, your taste buds have never achieved their full potential.'"

He untwists the hot fudge jar's lid and puts the jar in the microwave.

"Before you came along," he says, continuing his chitchat with the radio, "do you know how the bigshot astronaut was going to spend his last night on Earth? Drinking cocoa, eating an entire of pan of brownies dressed in a gallon of ice cream and hot fudge, and viewing a star show in the planetarium with some tunes on the juke then watching on my phone—my phone? Where did I put that? Not that I miss it, mind you, just curious where it went. Anyway, I was going to watch my favorite episode of *The Twilight Zone*, 'The Long Morrow,' the one about the astronaut who meets the woman of his dreams right when he is about to embark on a forty-year mission away from Earth—ain't that the way it goes?"

In the microwave, the fudge jar rotates through more seconds.

"I think I like old movies and old TV shows since I never met any of those actors—none of them came over for delicacies in our family's Hollywood hotbed—and I can still imagine them as decent people."

With two fingers, he pushes wet hair away from his forehead. "Dad would say, 'Fix your hair, you cocky little nothing.' Oh, those pet names from Jessie. He always has perfect hair."

He pats the mermaid's "hair" carved of stone.

"I hope I did buy spoons at some point. What do you think? Did I, or will this be a very messy night?"

The explorer opens a cabinet and smiles "Eureka" seeing a box of unopened silverware. He puts a spoon to use: first stirring milk and cocoa in the mug then dolloping chocolate ice cream onto the brownies.

"Sure, the brownies would be better if they were homemade, warm and oven-baked, you know, kissed by grandma or a wife or something Norman Rockwell like that, but I'm afraid a lifetime of being waited on by servants damaged by potential for domesticity," he confesses like he's revealing his deficits to a woman on a date.

BING—the microwave telling him the fudge is finished.

"I forced myself, in the name of living on my own, to learn how to use a microwave at least. Frankly, I like the hum of a microwave when my house is quiet—makes me imagine messages coming to Earth in the microwave frequency range. Is that weird? Look who I'm talking to—the weirdest radio around. We're both weird, that's it, don't feel bad, no one gets my messages either."

The fudge is *not* melted.

"Another fine how do ya do. The microwave isn't working either?"

He dollops clumps of thick un-melted fudge over ice cream and brownies then sticks the spoon like a flag into the "chocolate soil of the brownie planet."

"I sure wouldn't mind having some fettuccine alfredo from Bacio Dolce."

He takes another swig of medicine, allegedly capable of easing all aches associated with "colds."

"I wish had some chocolate chip pancakes, too, from that little pancake house in the south, Flapjack Fliers. Good eats."

He tries the microwave again and puts in the mug of cocoa. "I forgot to get marshmallows. Hot cocoa without marshmallows is like the night sky without stars."

Tick, tick, tick, the clock.

Nope, the cocoa won't heat either.

"Are microwaves not coming out? Fine. I'll drink *cold* chocolate milk. Apparently, I can't find a source of warmth tonight."

Finally, with his sweet dates in hand (cocoa milk and brownies), and radio snug under his arm, he goes into the sitting room, where he sits sock-footed and cross-legged on the gingerbread rug by the unheated fireplace. Brrrrr, he takes a moment to get the shiver out. God, it's so cold. He coughs again and again. The radio sits in front of him, the cup of cold chocolate milk beside him, and the brownie tin sits in his lap, where the brass compass chain dangles from belt loop to pocket.

"I did not buy a chair or a couch, as you can see. I had a plan to turn this planetarium into my home. There was going to be a big hearth, constructed of stone, with whopping blazes that could light and heat all the way into the library, where I'd read on cold snowy nights, amidst the crackle of fire, just like a monk or philosopher of yore. I'm not religious, mind you, but the solitary life of contemplation in a monastery is appealing, especially if the monastery is on a stony mountain, overlooking stars, sea, and Loch Ness monsters. Shouldn't there be science monks? Secular monks. You know, scientists and mathematicians and philosophers, who dedicate their lives to celibacy, quiet meditation, and quests for knowledge, freeing themselves from worldly distractions, focusing solely on thought. There could be a galactic network of these pondering monasteries and exchange programs amongst planets. Just imagine it: learning the knowledge of another world, their holiday traditions, enjoying recreational activities on this other planet like swimming in their seas…"

The aluminum tin sags from a hefty load of brownies and fudge and ice cream, and the astronaut takes a hearty bite of the gooey concoction.

"To heck with good breeding," the pedigreed golden boy asserts, while tossing out dinner table manners and devouring the brownies with the heartiness of a kid eating a bowl of sugary cereal on a Saturday morning. "So, in my science monastery, we wouldn't have austere rules about eating, though—chocolate would abound." His toes wiggle in his socks, just like a child on Christmas.

"I wish I could find my phone—turning on that episode of *The Twilight Zone* would make for good company. Not that the planetarium doesn't have good shows. Enjoying the stars' prettiness doesn't require comprehension of their being, but understanding their depths adds respect, awe, and a new layer to one's appreciation of the lights in the sky, don't you think? My plan was to put a mattress in the planetarium, so I could camp out under stars every night, regardless of weather, but you know what's missing from that scene? The sweetheart is missing, that's what, the one to hold in a romantic universe capable of snowflakes, shooting stars, and sweethearts! I don't know how anyone can think my spaceship is an ark that will save humanity—it requires *two* to continue the human species."

He turns on the radio, and the same sequence of songs floods out. The explorer ponders, while sipping cocoa, enjoying his chocolatey dinner before leaving Earth for the rest of his life.

"Why would any radio station continue playing the same snippets of songs?" He licks fudge off the side of his thumb. "No radio station would do that, of course; I had concluded that already. No radio station would leave a cocoa tin filled with a weird radio—no offense—out in the sea, with a message for 'Captain Elvin' to find either. So, where is the signal coming from?"

The heavy sleet doesn't answer.

The cold ice cream generates more goosebumps across him, so does the prospect of discovering an answer.

"What are you trying to tell me, radio?"

At the bottom of the aluminum tin, ice cream and fudge have turned into a syrupy soup full of bits of brownie crumbs, which "the monk" eats with the spoon.

"Maybe the message is in the songs' meanings?"

He admires the radio, which looks like a little heater, and now it's living up to its appearance—the music radiator is giving off its own special kind of warmth.

"Let's see, *Dear Prudence* implores someone to come out to play on a lovely day. *Star Tripper* realizes a trip to stardom doesn't compare with a trip to home. But the third and fourth songs don't seem to have any connection to my life."

The ponderer turns off the radio to contemplate, while finishing his meal.

"A message? Hmmmm…" He sets the empty brownie tin to the side. Keeping his boyhood manners, he wipes his lips with the back of his hand. "A message to Captain Elvin."

Stiff cold, he gets up to make more cocoa. The medicinal syrup hasn't helped his sore throat or his aches. He really wants to crawl into bed, a secret made known by his sluggishness.

"Captain Elvin, my boyhood secret identity—a galactic pen pal of sorts, at least in my fantasies."

He taps his reddened fingers atop the counter and alternates between staring at Rosetta and the limestone mermaid.

"'Dear alien,' I used to call out to anyone in the stars willing to listen. 'I, Captain Elvin, am sending out this message in a space bottle to find a friend from another world. Write back and we'll be pen pals in the stars.'"

Reminiscing, he stirs more cocoa in the cup.

"And I'd send up tiny rockets with notes attached, or I'd flash Morse Code beams of light, as if extraterrestrials could understand that. *Dear alien…*"

BINGO flashes across the explorer's eyes!

"*Dear*—is that it? The song *titles* spell out the message?"

He takes pen and pad of stationary from the counter and goes back to the sitting room to sit beside the radio.

"Dear Prudence, Star Tripper? Or just Dear, Star Tripper? That's it, isn't it? Your message begins, 'Dear, Star Tripper.'"

After more reflecting and sipping of cold cocoa, the scientist realizes not all words in the message are in the song title but in the lyrics, and some words must be construed through reason, such as words like "the" and "a." After writing everything down, the radio astronomer takes time to grasp what he has deciphered:

Dear Star Tripper,
You have spent your life calling aliens. Now it is time to pick up the phone because one is calling you. I am a visitor to this planet. But, like you, I will soon be leaving Earth. My last hours on this world would be blessed if they could be fulfilled in your company, especially during this Earthly holiday season. If you will grant me this meeting, please respond through telepathy as I am adept at such communication, as are you, if you are willing to remember.

How utterly bizarre, his face expresses…yet…fascinating.

He stands up and paces slowly like a lecturer, trying to make a complex subject make sense.

More goosebumps, more goosebumps, more goosebumps.

"If not for the Captain Elvin thing, and the fact that you know my secret language, and the fact you're transmitting a signal from God knows where, I'd think you were a hoax," he says to the little radio standing on rug. "But I also can't believe you're what you say you are either—a message from an alien on Earth, soon to be vacating this planet and just wanting to spend the holidays with me. How entirely precious. Yes, I'd think the one who made your message was a gold-digger, or fame digger, or reporter, or loon set to assassinate the space program, but …. how could you know things about me no one knows, no one has ever had access to knowing, unless … it's just too fantastical … unless you are truly adept at telepathy. Well, telepathy isn't completely out of scientific possibility, although," he says snappishly, while he shoots a stare of suspicion at the radio, "being skilled in telepathy doesn't mean you're an alien. You could have a talent for telepathy and still be one of those devious characters I already mentioned, using your telepathic skills to bamboozle me. Or … or …" His cold suspicion melting on the radio's warmth. "You could contain a message from that fabulous creature I encountered in the sea all those years ago? Ah, it's just ridiculous!"

By the cobbled wall, he sinks back down, his knees up against his cold chest, and he feels his own heartbeat tapping against his kneecap.

"Well, if you are a gold-digger, or fame digger, or reporter, what harm could you do me? None. I'll be gone soon and I'm never coming back. And if you're an assassin, I doubt you'd resort to something as absurd as leaving me a message in a radio. I doubt anyone would do that, because it's too … well, sweet, charming, interesting, and the come-on lines never are. Plus, I'm not that hard to find. My whereabouts constantly tracked by media, photos of my home plastered in magazines, my speeches publicized."

The "science monk" rests his cold chin against his knee, taps it up and down a few times, trying to tap out a decision.

"Telepathy. Sure. I could try." With his fingertip, he pats the quiet little radio, pretty in her own way. "Here goes: Meet me here, at the Sandra Horn Planetarium, tonight." He closes his eyes, as if that makes his telepathic powers stronger, losing at least one sense of this interfering world, and he continues to contact the messenger…

~~~~~~

After the telepathy experiment, the astronomer opens the door to "the universe," continuing with his original plan to enjoy a star show with tunes on the old-timey jukebox. Holding cocoa mug and radio, he clasps the Mars-red suitcase under his arm. He still can't locate his phone.

The explorer walks into the planetarium on socked feet and flicks on the stage lights with the side of his elbow, but the shadowy auditorium seats remain in darkness.

The theater, feeling as cold as outer space, is quiet except for the tick tock of the clock in the other room, and sleet, popping against the roof like meteorites bombarding a spacecraft. The black dome ceiling is a half-sphere like the night sky. At stage right, three carpeted steps lead to a black-carpeted stage in the semi-round, or crescent-moon shape; another set of steps lead up to center stage, where lies an open sleeping bag the tarnished tan color of an old treasure map. Atop the sleeping bag are a brown, sherpa blanket and a naked pillow, laid out beside a 1940s, round-top jukebox plugged into a socket in the floor. The astronomer sets the radio and suitcase beside the jukebox and sets the cocoa mug by the sleeping bag. Beyond the carpeted stage, the floor is black brick and speckled white (just like the carpet) to create the illusion of a starfield, a *rough* starfield to prevent shoes from sliding. An otherworldly-looking star projector stands close to first-row seats.

In his own private universe, the astronaut turns on the planetarium's show, "Phenomena of the Universe." He complements the star show with Jackson Browne's *Late for the Sky.* Camped out on the sleeping bag, hands behind his head, he watches shooting stars ride across the fake sky, which looks real enough to please him. Comets, supernova, the show has it all, except *her.* He pulls the brown blanket onto him and shivers in it.

The astronaut hears a noise, loud enough to reach over the wall of song. Surely just ice on the roof. But it sounded like a small thud, like something falling onto brick flooring. He pulls off the blanket, stands up, and turns off the music. He was not hired to be an astronaut for startling easily. His heart rate rarely accelerates, so say the records from
~~~~~~

numerous spaceflight medical exams. His brain stays logical, so confirm the tests taken under extreme and bewildering circumstances. Calmly, he walks to the edge of the stage like a captain called to the bridge to examine a perplexing sight in the sea. The astronaut has stood face to face with polar bears in the arctic; scorpions have crawled into his sleeping bag in desert isolation; meteorites have hurled past him in space; his tether rope once detached from spaceship and almost left him stranded from his mother planet for a lifetime, yet…

The astronaut – "Is someone out there?"

A voice across the universe, "Yes."

The explorer puts the side of his hand above his brow like a sailor in salute, shielding his eyes from stage lights. He sees a small silhouetted figure in the depths of obscurity, back row. The silhouette is paused, mid-way leaning down, as if reaching for whatever fell that made the noise, but the being was caught in the process of retrieval like a burglar who is warned, "Hands up!"

The astronaut wouldn't make much of an explorer of the *unknown* if he was scared of seeing figures in the dark, yet…

The astronaut – "What are you doing in here?"

Why did he sound so hostile, so accusatory—is that the tone he'd use with a being from space? No, just with nosy beings from this world, as any prying reporter will confirm.

The silhouette sits upright and no doubt sees the character on stage, lit up in lights—he is standing in defensive stance, hands on his hips, while a comet hurtles across the sky.

The voice in the depths – "Please, don't hurt me. I'll be leaving unless..."

The voice sounds small, frightened, female, the way a doe would sound begging a hunter not to shoot her.

The astronaut – "I'm sorry. I'm not going to hurt you."

The being is short, the astronaut can tell that, and maybe bald? The explorer makes out what looks like a stick, or a cane, slanted against a seat next to the silhouetted figure.

The winter storm must have covered up the sound earlier but now he hears what sounds like peculiar breathing from a being who has adapted a different strategy for inhaling.

The astronaut – "I just meant, who are you?"

The voice in the depths – "If you don't know then…"

Again, the words sound crouched, hiding behind a quiet voice and trying not to be too conspicuous.

The "breathing" sound may be coming from some kind of photographic equipment. That surely irks the private star, but he puts on a press conference smile and tone.

The astronaut – "If you're a paparazzo—"

The voice in the depths – "I am not a papa-raz-zo."

The astronaut – "Ah, really?"

Still accusatory.

The astronaut – "Well, you'll have plenty of chances tomorrow to get my picture, but I deserve to spend my last night on Earth away from all that."

The voice in the depths – "I was mistaken."

On the word "mistaken," it sounds like something breaks inside her.

The voice in the depths – "I'll leave. Please, let me."

The little voice sounds shaky on conversation like talking with someone is an earthquake that shakes her foundation, and if she has to speak for too long, she'll crumble.

How does he know that about her?

Tick, tick, tick the clock, warning the astronaut his time on Earth is passing by.

The astronaut – "Wait. I'm just curious. How did you get in here?"

The voice in the depths – "The door was open and…"

The astronaut looks at the emergency door in the far back of the planetarium. The sign above of the door flashes red like a sign above a hatch in a spaceship.

The astronaut – "*And?*"

The voice in the depths – "Please, just let me leave in peace and let me take my bric-a-brac."

Bric-a-brac? The astronaut looks around and notices a wooden suitcase the color of pine, shellacked shiny, and a bulky, tattered, black knapsack that looks as old as Robin Hood's era, and a shawl as blue as nightfall sitting by the stage. All of the stuff is damp from rain; sleet crystals are melting on the shawl and knapsack.

The astronaut – "Is this your stuff up here?"

The voice in the depths – "Yes. I will go now."

He strains to hear her small voice across the expanse, especially since it's lost in the pelting ice and rowdy thunder.

The astronaut – "Of course you're free to leave."

The voice in the depths – "Please leave the room first so that I may retrieve my belongings in privacy."

Every word sounds thought out, as if spoken by a voice unfamiliar with language and speaking, remembering (or learning) how to properly use conversation.

The astronaut – "Leave the room? I'm the owner of this here universe."

The voice in the depths – "What?"

The being seems so serious like she belongs in his monastery of quiet contemplation.

The astronaut – "I own this planetarium. Listen, I promise I'm not going to hurt you. You can come up here and get your stuff. I just want to know why you're here. Autograph seeker? One-night seeker? Reporter? Militant who wants to shoot me to end space exploration?"

The voice in the depths – "End space exploration? Why would I want to do that?"

The voice is so frail it sounds breakable, too frail to be in a body strong enough to do much fighting with anyone. The peculiar noise emanating from her direction does not sound like photography equipment but labored breathing.

The voice in the depths – "I only wanted a hiatus from the cold. I have nowhere else to go, until I finally leave for good. That is all."

The astronaut – "Are you telling me the truth?"

The voice in the depths – "Not exactly, but may I leave?"

The astronaut – "It's a free planet, partially at least. What did you mean 'not exactly' and 'leave for good'?"

Is the astronaut planning on grilling aliens in this *Dragnet* style of police interrogation?

The star sneezes, big and loud enough to shame his mother.

The voice in the depths: "You're sick."

An underlying warmth in her tone says, "Let me make you some warm soup." Doesn't it?

The astronaut – "It's just a little cold."

The voice in the depths – "If you will not leave the room, will you turn around while I get my belongings?"

The astronaut – "Why? Are you going to shoot me, either with a gun or a lens?"

The voice in the depths – "I don't want *you* to chase me away."

Chase her away?

The astronaut's face suggests irritation has dissipated and been replaced with curiosity. He is a scientist, a cosmic detective, and he has come upon an interesting mystery in this universe, especially … well, especially since he just sent out a telepathic message for an alien to meet him in this planetarium.

Shooting stars stream across the black sky like tinsel, while ice gallops along the roof, sounding fantastical now like reindeer galloping in the Christmastime night.

The figure leans down and retrieves whatever fell to the floor. In doing so, the breathing sound ceases. The room is quiet again, except for sleet and bawdy thunder, which sounds capable of shattering the outside sky but not the planetarium's sky.

The astronaut – "You shouldn't go out in that storm."

The voice in the depths – "Why do you say that?"

Her voice is somewhat louder now as if it has been given a shot of "voice booster."

The astronaut – "Because it could be dangerous, out here on a slippery steep mountain in pouring ice in pitch dark nighttime and fog."

An underlying warmth in *his* tone says, "Stay here, please." Doesn't it?

The voice in the depths – "Are you saying you care if I'm in danger?"

The astronaut – "Sure, I don't want anyone to be in danger."

The voice in the depths – "Are you telling *me* the truth?"

The astronaut – "Is it so hard to believe?"

The voice in the depths – "Yes, from a human, yes."

The astronaut – "From a human?"

The voice in the depths – "But maybe you're not…"

The being doesn't finish her thought, and her silhouette is still.

The astronaut – "Please tell me what you meant."

The voice in the depths - "Humans have never worried about my being in danger. If you tell me you truly care about my safety, I'll be inclined to believe you're an angel, not a man, that you're…"

Again, she doesn't finish her sentence.

The astronaut – "The only wings I'll ever get are on a spacecraft. Tell me, why do you refer to 'humans' as something you're not?" His voice turns as defensive as a man against a shark. "Wait. You're an alien, eh? Sure. For a moment, I believed you really were a lost soul just seeking shelter from the storm. But, now, I see what's really going on here. I don't know if someone put you up to this joke, someone from the space agency maybe, one last joke on 'that cocky jerk,' or maybe it was good ol' Jessie getting one last jab at his son, or maybe you're just trying to feed me the most original line—"

The voice in the depths – "What do you mean? *Line*? Joke? I've heard nothing funny said between us."

The astronaut – "It's funny that you're trying to make me, the 'alientologist,' believe you're an alien."

The voice in the depths – "Do you think it's funny to be a foreigner on this planet, always chased away, never welcomed anywhere? Never even granted the common human courtesy of 'Hello, how are you?' Everyone is a reminder of my loneliness—another one I don't belong with."

What if … what if the being really is what the space program will be traveling lightyears from Earth to discover?

The astronaut – "A foreigner? Where are you from?"

The voice in the depths– "I'm going to leave. I thought—do nevermind."

The astronaut – "Wait."

The voice in the depths – "Why? You think I am a joke."

The astronaut – "I didn't say that. I said I thought you were trying to joke me. I don't know what to think."

The voice in the depths – "I don't either. I do. But I'm just not sure now."

The explorer sits on the side of the stage, his socked feet dangling. His eyes search for her across the darkness. She is still sitting quietly in the back row.

The astronaut – "What do you mean, you're just not sure now?"

He moves his toes up and down, and the fabric Jupiters on his brown socks wiggle.

The voice in the depths – "I better come out with it because I may never get another chance—I thought it was *you*, at first, when you turned on the stars. But I was afraid, I admit, of speaking up and directing you to my presence. Then when you snapped, I thought perhaps you were someone else—one of those menacing security people always lurking about. Then when you said it was your last night on Earth, I knew it was you. I had sensed it anyway, yet I was still mistaken."

Again, something cracks inside her on the word "mistaken"; perhaps something delicate like a wish.

The astronaut – "I'm sorry but I don't know what you're talking about."

The voice in the depths – "I knew you would visit The Wedded Islets before leaving this planet."

Up to this moment, the explorer's voice has been calm and "sitting down," and now it jumps up, a high pitch up to the ceiling:

The astronaut – "How do you know they're called *The Wedded Islets*? I made that up!"

The voice in the depths – "Yes, I know. You're the one who tied the rope around their bases as a symbol of their eternal love. You were a child when you created the legend about the married rocks after reading the book *The Dream of the Red Chamber*, or *The Story of the Stone*. You were so charmed by that idea—of a sentient stone—you saw the rocks as alive. You think the wife rock looks shy. I've always felt the same about the rocks. Many moons I've slept on the bosom of the wife rock, and many sunrises I've caught sunlight atop the husband rock, and many sunsets I've perched on The Wedded Islets with a wish in my soul."

The astronaut hasn't blinked once while listening to her incredible explanation, as if the explanation is something he can see and doesn't want to miss any detail.

The voice in the depths – "Like me, you're a romance preservationist, so I knew you would tighten the bonding rope between the stones before you left Earth. That was why I placed the radio there for you. I put the radio in a cocoa tin because you love cocoa, and I placed the message in the radio because a radio is tangible. I thought you, the scientist, would be more willing to believe the message hearing it that way than if I had just sent the songs by way of telepathy, since you've become very skeptical of things you once believed in childhood."

The sailor's eyes get wider and wider, as if he's watching a magnificent creature swimming closer and closer to his spaceship's porthole.

The voice in the depths – "I watched you go beneath the sea. Then you got lost in the fog. But when you turned on the radio, I felt the big beat of your excited heart inside me, and that was my cue to send the flood of song snippets to your mind, telepathically. I felt you would like that: deciphering the code. I thought you had received my message, Captain Elvin, and you had sent one back to me to be here in this planetarium tonight. But I must have misperceived, which happens on occasions, especially around one so guarded, guarded even to himself. That must be why I am having difficulty reading you. I am receiving conflicting feelings from my intuition because *you* are confused and conflicted. Well, I do hope I did not misperceive everything."

She says it so matter of fact—"Oh, I thought you reached out to me telepathically, but I was mistaken, that's all"!

The astronaut's heart rate accelerates now, a heart secret visible in the reddening of his face like lava glowing beneath charcoaled rock.

The astronaut – "I must've drunk more of that cough syrup than I thought. Or I'm cracking, finally, the grand scientist has lost all his marbles. No, she's a figment of my imagination. 'A crumb of cheese, a fragment of underdone potato,' as Ebenezer Scrooge would say. It is Christmastime after all, good setting for a stage of *A Christmas Carol.* I need some hot chocolate."

He stands up quickly, pads over to the cocoa mug.

The voice in the depths – "Yes, you love chocolate, that I was not mistaken about then."

The astronaut – "Anyone could know I love chocolate. Doesn't require telepathy. Just a subscription to *Newsweek*."

The being doesn't combat his attack on her sincerity but stays peaceful in the back row.

The voice in the depths—"Does it only require a subscription to … *Newsweek* … to know you sent out a telepathic message to me just an hour ago, Captain Elvin?"

The astronaut – "*How could you know*—" He clears his throat. Must have been the chocolate drink that made his voice sound so girlishly high-pitched. The Top Gun deepens his voice back to manly *baritone*; he's never been a *bass* like his dad. "Why do you call me Captain Elvin?"

The voice in the depths – "Because that's what you call yourself. Or am I wrong about that? I'm afraid telepathy does have glitches. 'Elvin' means 'old friend,' does it not? You still consider yourself an old friend to the aliens you always tried to reach out to as a child with your messages to space; inside, you still see yourself as Captain Elvin, a star sailor, captain of your own spaceboat, the way you saw yourself when you were a small boy."

The astronaut sits back on the stage's edge with his mug of cold cocoa.

The voice in the depths – "I can make it warm for you. I'll try to anyway."

The astronaut – "What?"

The voice in the depths – "I haven't practiced this in a while. But I'll send a signal to your mind that the chocolate drink is warm, so you'll perceive it as warm."

The astronaut says to himself, "This is nuts, this is absolutely mixed nuts of all varieties, not the average peanut kind of nuts but all-out walnut kind of crazy. I must have said that Captain Elvin thing to somebody, sometime, that's it." To the being in the depths, he says, "Hey, it didn't necessarily require a telepathic connection to me to know about Captain Elvin. I wrote that down sometimes on my messages."

The voice in the depths – "Are you speaking to me? I do not hear well anymore, I'm afraid, nor see well."

The astronaut – "I'm sorry to hear that."

The voice in the depths – "Do you mean that?"

The astronaut – "Use your telepathy and find out."

The voice in the depths – "I sense you do mean it but you do not realize you do mean it … but maybe … that is my own wishful thinking that you care. Sometimes telepathy is blurred by wishful thinking. I'll turn off my telepathy if you feel it is an invasion of your privacy."

The astronaut – "Apparently, you've been invading it for years now. Why did you do this—the radio, the message, breaking in here?"

The voice in the depths – "Because I thought you needed this as much as I. Some are lonely of body—they desire a physical entwinement. Some are lonely of mind—they yearn for an intellectual union. And some are lonely of heart—they crave an emotional bond. But some of us are lonely much deeper inside."

The astronaut – "Listen, I'm leaving tomorrow, and I can't fulfill whatever fantasy you may be having."

The voice in the depths – "What fantasy am I having? Now, use *your* telepathy to answer."

The astronaut – "One of the fantasies they all have."

The voice in the depths – "*They*?"

The astronaut – "The gold-diggers, fame seekers, the ones who feel a 'special' bond with the so-called handsome face on the magazines."

The voice in the depths – "Did you use your telepathy to arrive at that answer?"

The astronaut – "No, I used inductive reasoning—a series of encounters with those types I just mentioned led me to this generalized conclusion."

The voice in the depths – "I told you in my message, Captain Elvin, I am a tourist on this planet, a no one to your world, and I'm leaving Earth as well. I do not seek gold or fame, which are completely useless where I'm going, and I cannot see much of your handsome face—I have never been able to see your face completely. You are just an outline of a blur with blue eyes. Now I am losing my sight completely."

The astronaut – "If you're being honest, I'm sorry. About you losing your sight."

The voice in the depths – "Don't trust me on my word. Feel it. You have the ability to feel whether I am telling the truth. You called me here tonight with your thoughts."

The astronaut – "That's completely crazy."

He stands up again as a way to add an exclamation point to his sentence.

The voice in the depths – "Try your drink."

The astronaut picks up the mug by the handle, eyes it like it may be poisonous, but decides to take a chance and sip it. "It's warm!" He sets the mug back down as if it's filled with little bogeymen. "And it tastes even better than hot cocoa from Chocolate Truffle Inn!"

The voice in the depths – "Thank you. My own special recipe. There's nothing magical in the cup for you to be scared of. The perception of warmth and taste is coming from your own mind. You believed the cocoa would be warm and delicious and therefore it is. Now use your telepathy to feel who I am."

The astronaut – "Stop saying that. I don't have any telepathic abilities."

The voice in the depths – "Then how did I know to be here? I admit I did set out before I got your message to meet you here. I knew you would come here. And I had the hope that you would summon me here after deciphering my radio message."

The astronaut – "Anyone could know I own this planetarium, and although I don't think most would guess I'd be spending my last night here, it's not out of the realm of possibility for someone to guess that, especially if someone goaded me with a strange message in a radio to invite them over. I don't know how you did the radio trick—"

The voice in the depths – "No trick. Just telepathy."

The astronaut – "What do you mean?"

He sits back down and gazes into the darkness, trying to really see who is out there.

The voice in the depths – "Only *you* can hear those song snippets from the radio, Captain Elvin. If anyone else turned the radio on it would only spout blank air. Like I explained, I didn't need to use the radio at all to send you a telepathic message, but I thought you would appreciate the convention since you are a radio astronomer, who has hoped, his entire life, to discover a message in a space bottle."

The astronaut – "But I listened to the message more than once. How could you have known when I was listening to it to send me the exact same message, the exact same song snippets over and over?"

The voice in the depths – "I only had to send the message once, when I felt, through intuition, you had turned on the radio for the first time. You enjoy figuring out mysteries. I knew you would continue trying to solve the puzzle in songs. The other times you turned on the radio, your own mind supplied the message—a message which intrigued you, a message you wanted to receive, did you not? On the beach, I also sang, only for you to hear, *The Mermaid's Song* and the Christmas carol, which I thought you would enjoy since you love music. *Late for the Sky*, isn't that the song you listen to in orbit?"

The astronaut – "I could test you on your telepathic abilities."

The voice in the depths – "Okay but I thought you wanted me to turn off my telepathy."

The astronaut – "What number am I thinking of?"

The voice in the depths – "9."

The astronaut – "Lucky guess. What's the square root of .121472?"

The voice in the depths – "Knowing the answer to that doesn't require telepathy, but I do perceive that you don't know the answer either, so I'm drawing a blank. I'm not a math whiz. I'm a telepath."

The astronaut – "What was my goldfish's name when I was a kid?"

The voice in the depths – "I'm searching your mind and I sense no memories of a goldfish ever being in your life, so I'm guessing you were trying to stump me on a trick question. In fact, you think it's cruel to trap a fish in a bowl, as do I, because we are seafarers, you and I, and we respect the sea's lifeforms and their freedom. You don't sail your boat at Mach 7; you sail slowly like a man finally making love to a girl he loves and savoring every ripple of blissful contact. I'm sorry, I know that embarrasses you. Despite your playboy reputation, you are a gentleman who blushes at crudeness. In childhood, you enjoyed making model ships and miniature sailboats, voyaging them across the starry nighttime ocean, while imagining the universe as a sea and hoping to canoe the rapids of the 'white water' Milky Way. You even made up your own constellation, The Mermaid. You hope to spot a mermaid, who lives in a sea of stars, a mermaid waiting to encounter the star sailor and invite him to her world. You are wishing the world you'll be traveling toward is not *unknown* but *familiar* to you—your true world, your shared world with her. You remind me of a little boy right now, sitting on the edge of the stage like it is a pier and letting your feet wade through air, hoping the special mermaid will tug on your toe to join her for a swim. Is my intuition right or wrong?"

The astronaut, puzzled yet captivated by the puzzle – "Who are you?"

The voice in the depths – "If you use your intuition, you'll know who I am."

The astronaut – "Are you really not a reporter or autograph seeker?"

The voice in the depths – "I have no profession on this planet. If you need further proof of my telepathic abilities, I know inside your red suitcase is your collection of rocks, or as you call it, 'your rock family,' which you have been assembling since boyhood and it is the only thing from Earth you care to take with you on your long journey. Another passion I share, although most of the rocks I've found came from the sea. I know that you once lived in a small spaceship that had food, toilet, computer for reading and writing, and cot for sleeping and dreaming, because the space agency was testing to see if you would go insane by yourself, but aside from the physical smallness of the room, nothing had changed for you, except you missed your rock family. Like me, you have always felt contained in a small spaceship, voyaging this world alone."

The astronaut has lost interest in *The Twilight Zone* on TV because he has entered it in reality. He unlocks his trust, frees it for the moment.

The astronaut – "Alright, I'll play along for fun and assume you are an *alien* who sent me a telepathic message to meet you. For an alien, you know our language pretty well."

The alien – "I have learned. For a scientist, you are very vain."

The astronaut – "What?"

The alien – "You assume everyone is out for your picture or autograph."

The astronaut – "Ah."

The alien – "I did not mean to be funny at you."

The astronaut – "*At* me?"

The alien – "To be cruel, I mean, by calling you vain. I'm very sorry. I sense it hurt you more than you've let on. But you should not let vanity barricade you from important meetings."

The astronaut – "It's not vanity."

The alien – "What is it?"

The astronaut – "You're the telepath, you tell me."

The alien – "*Fear* prevents you from meeting new people. In fact, you are more afraid that I'm human than alien. But I understand. Humans have been both mean and non-understanding towards you. So, you are very guarded, as am I. You hide your inner boy behind sarcasm, after letting people inside who only ridiculed your quirky interior for being at odds with your beautiful exterior."

The astronaut steps off the stage and sits on the arm of a front row seat.

The astronaut – "I can hear you better if I'm closer."

The alien - "That's close enough for now." *Fear* undisguised in her small voice. "Whereas you station guards around your interior self, I am more guarded with my outer self, not wanting anyone to see me, but I've always dreamed of giving a tour of the interior and someone deciding to take residence with me."

The astronaut – "So when are you leaving?"

The alien – "Not too long from now, just like you."

The astronaut – "That's why you're traveling with a suitcase and bag?"

The alien – "No, I use the suitcase and bag on land, in this world. I won't be needing it where I'm travelling."

The astronaut – "What's inside the suitcase?"

The alien – "Why do you ask? Because you sense something interesting is in the case?"

The astronaut – "I was just curious."

The alien – "Use your telepathy."

The astronaut – "I don't have any."

Yet, a vision comes into his mind of…an accordion?

The alien – "The box contains two cameras."

The astronaut (all the locks back in place) – "Cameras!? I thought you said you were not a photographer, that you had no profession on this planet."

He stands up in the aisle, turns away from the path that leads to her, and goes back up to the stage.

Tick, tick, tick, the clock…

The alien – "A profession is a task one gets paid in dollars to do. I get paid nothing. I am a tourist who travels with a camera. Please trust me. For years, I have snuck around on land, snapping shots of this world, sights like The Wedded Islets to take home with me, but as I mentioned, now I am losing my sight completely."

The astronaut – "Do you mind if I see the cameras?"

He picks up the suitcase.

The alien – "I do not mind. I enjoy sharing these aspects of me with you, Captain Elvin."

The explorer sits on the stage, and like a kid opening a treasure chest, he opens the wooden box.

The alien – "Forgive me for using my telepathy but I can't help sense that you have the same feeling you had as a boy when you found a secret compartment in a Christmas music box that you had rescued from a garbage bin, and you discovered the secret drawer was filled with forlorn love poems written by a lonely different gal from a long time ago, wishing for her true love for the holidays, and you wanted to build a time machine to go to her and give her a gift."

The astronaut – "Yes, I was wal-nuts back then too, obsessed with fantastical love stories. I can't believe I just told you that but I suppose you already knew it."

The alien – "And I like it. Being embarrassed by the romantic property of yourself is like a rainbow being embarrassed by its colors."

The astronaut – "Rainbows are seen as kind of corny and childish in today's world."

The alien – "And that makes you as sad as it makes me."

The astronaut – "*It Came Upon the Midnight Clear* played in the music box, and that's why you sang it on the beach, eh?"

The alien – "Yes."

Inside the suitcase are an old-timey camera with an *accordion* body, and a waterproof camera for underwater photography, and a few slides are in the box too, along with an assortment of discarded seashells and rocks—dingy ones, shiny ones, colorful ones.

The alien – "Maybe we can combine our rock family."

The astronaut – "Yeah, I'll adopt your rock children and you'll adopt mine."

They both laugh, which adds a bit of holiday cheer to the scene.

The sailor puts a large conch next to his ear.

The astronaut – "Sounds like the sea is inside of me."

The alien – "I do that too, whenever I'm on land."

The astronaut – "I'm also a photographer of sorts. At UBF, I work on aperture synthesis imaging—a way of taking images of the sky from many different perspectives."

The alien – "Yes, you can see that the galaxy's shadowed heart glows immensely bright if seen with the right lens."

The astronaut – "That was a refreshingly poetic way to describe my research."

The alien – "Thank you."

The astronaut – "Thank you."

The alien – "Maybe there are emissions from the Milky Way's core that will never be detected with eyes or ears or any equipment because all of Earth's equipment was designed for *human* senses to read."

The astronaut – "I wonder that too."

It came upon the midnight clear,
that glorious song of old,
from angels bending near the earth
to touch their harps of gold

The astronaut – "My apologies for the cliché but you have the voice of an angel."

The alien – "So do you."

The astronaut – "I'm not much of a singer, except in the shower—have you been spying on me in there?"

The alien – "No! I meant angels say kind things like 'You have the voice of an angel,' therefore you speak with the voice of an angel."

The astronaut – "Tell that to my colleagues, give them a good laugh."

The alien – "Then they don't know the real you."

The star picks up a lens from the camera box.

The astronaut – "Ah, a telephoto lens, not used for close-ups of the soul but close-ups of a zit. Oh, the joys of fame."

The alien – "Tell me how you feel about it."

She feels like his girl, asking about him, his life, his feelings, on an intense journey towards Coupledome, during this one-of-a-kind holiday date.

The astronaut – "About fame? Let's see…I was born on Ascension Day, and Mother wanted me to be so famous, that day would be commemorated as *my* birthday, more important than Christ's ascension to Heaven." He laughs at the absurdity.

The alien – "You were born on Ascension Day and I was born on any old Tuesday."

The astronaut – "Do they have 'Tuesdays' on your world?"

The alien – "I was using Earthspeak to make the point that I am not renowned, or significant to anyone, except…maybe…"

The astronaut has the feeling that the alien has accomplished no feat on this world, or any world, other than the longest meditation, but no Earthling knows about her feat of transcendence. No, wait, she has accomplished an incredible feat—of crafting a compassionate heart, like a ruby formed under immense pressure, and maintaining its delicate crystalline beauty in a world with heart bulldozers. How does he know she has a prism of a heart that uses rain to form a rainbow? He senses it. Maybe—no, it's too crazy—but maybe he shares that phantastic, telepathic gene Z?

He sets the suitcase on the stage.

The astronaut - "My mother once said, 'How do you know when you've reached the peak of fame? When you become a dream symbol. When a psychologist says having *you* in a dream is a symbol for –fill in the blank for whatever you represent—.' A dream symbol, not even a real person."

The alien – "And what do you represent in a dream?"

The astronaut – "You tell me. What would I represent in your dream?"

He walks over to the edge of the stage as if ready to dive back into this moment of getting to know her.

The alien – "What would I represent in yours?"

The astronaut – "Honestly?"

The alien – "I'll try to take whatever you say."

The astronaut – "It's not anything bad. In a dream, I'd wish you were real. There, I said it."

The alien – "That was very kind. Thank you. See, you have the voice of an angel."

He's never heard a more grateful "thank you" like he gave her the grandest present.

The alien – "Why would you want *me* to be real?"

The astronaut – "As you already know, when I was a kid, I sometimes stayed up all night fantasizing about encountering a being from another world."

The alien – "If you were in my dream, I'd wish you were real too."

The astronaut – "Because I'm a star?"

The alien – "Yes but not the kind you're referring to. You are carved from stars, we all are."

The astronaut – "Tell that to my mother. Being a star is my birthright."

The alien – "Like me, I sense you care more about your lineage from starlight than your worldly genetics, and you never cared about the stars on the red carpet, only the ones in the sky. But you once tried to use fame for acceptance from this planet, until you realized the astronaut was *well-known* but no one knew *you* at all. You got trapped by competition, society's gravity, and now you want to fly free of that. You want a rest from pretending, a respite from the race to the peak of stardom—you just want to slowly sail the cosmic ocean, Captain Elvin, and take in all its sights, along with a kindred shipmate."

The star walks off the stage and goes back to sitting on the arm of a first-row seat, turned toward the back row.

The astronaut – "Perhaps you're right. I see the error of my ways now."

The alien – "Do you? You're still looking for a home in history books, a home you've found nowhere else on this planet. Your words have been translated in every language on Earth, yet no one understands *your* language, do they, Captain Elvin?"

The astronaut – "But you do?"

The alien – "Didn't I write a message to you in your own language?"

Silence, except for the sleeting sky and ticking clock. She has handed out the rope to pull him closer to her, but it's up to the sailor to grab on or founder in the dark waters of alone-ness.

The astronaut – "What's inside the knapsack?"

The alien – "Mostly everything I own on this planet. Just some old clothes, the camouflage needed for blending into human society when I go on shore."

The astronaut – "Amphibious, are you? Part-time landlubber, part-time ocean dweller?"

The alien – "Part-time star dweller. Like you."

The explorer looks out at her and sees that the "cane," leaning against the seat, looks like a wooden baseball bat painted black. A vision comes into his mind from the alien's point of view: she always keeps the knapsack, suitcase, and Louisville Slugger close by in case she needs a quick getaway. She hides her odd form beneath the shawl. Accepted nowhere on Earth, the alien is shooed away from everywhere, sometimes by force.

The astronaut – "Would you like some hot chocolate?"

Has she ever been offered any?

The alien – "I'm afraid I have no stomach for hot chocolate."

The astronaut – "Do you mean literally?"

The alien – "Use your telepathy."

The astronaut – "I don't need telepathy. I have logic. You didn't mean literally."

The alien – "When you are barbed, it makes me recede."

The astronaut – "My apologies."

The alien – "You don't need barbs around me. I'd never harm you. You can look in the bag, if you like. I'm beginning to believe my trust in you is valid."

The astronaut – "Why?"

The alien – "I feel it."

The journeyer goes over to the ancient knapsack. Without opening it, he sees that inside are old, thready clothes and a bar of soap the color of butter. The soap also functions as shampoo. It smells medicine-ish like a Band-Aide. But the old saying fits, "Beggars can't be choosers." He has a vision of the buoyant soap floating on the sea, where the alien bathes in foamy suds so cold it feels like solid ice sheets. The coldness makes her breathing even more labored. Why doesn't the amphibious creature swim away to warmer seas?

As if empathizing with her coldness, he coughs, shivers, rubs his arms for warmth.

The alien – "You and I have adapted to coldness. Like me, you grew up in a cold place; even when it wasn't cold, it was cold."

The astronaut – "True. I was born in the Antarctic, but I tell you my parents' mansion in Hollowwood, also known as Hollywood, was colder, even though it's in a 'nice' neighborhood—the houses are 'nice' if not the people. Even moving to the beach didn't add warmth to our house. It wasn't a home. A house is a structure where one resides, but a *home* is something more, I think."

The alien – "I do too."

He sits again on the chair's arm.

The astronaut – "My childhood house was more suitable for a robot kid than a human kid, very modern and electronic and cold, not homey."

The alien – "I'm sorry that your childhood house was never a home."

The astronaut – "Every cocktail party is just a press conference, everyone putting on their image. The cocktail mansion is always crowded with humans as plastic and pretty as the fruit, hiding the rot inside. I was always lonely for loneliness. I was strange. I often skipped school to learn, started fights to avoid fights, and ran away from home to find a home. I always thought I was going to run up to the North Pole, and all I needed was Polaris, the sky's compass."

The alien – "Like me, you love Earth's animals, but you are never invited into their homes either—they go into their burrows and you're left outside."

The astronaut – "And I wasn't allowed to have a dog or cat when I was a kid since Jessie was supposedly allergic to dogs and cats and niceness all around!"

He senses the alien has no home on Earth. Homeless, the alien lives, when she's on shore, in an old sweater, discarded junk she found during her Terra travels. Houses protect one from the elements, and since she doesn't have a house, clothing serves as walls to protect her body from weather when she is on land. Worrying about finding *matching* clothes is immaterial when you're just looking for efficient cloth to guard you from inhospitable climates. The layering technique—cardigan sweater, button down, T-shirt—is used to control the thermostat. Opening the sweater is like opening a window on a hot day, buttoning it is like turning on the heater in winter. But unlike doors and windows, clothes don't have locks, so she has two forms of protection against intruders: to run and swim away and to swing the baseball bat, but her compassionate heart never chooses the latter choice.

The alien – "Please have some more hot chocolate. Would you like it with peppermint to soothe your throat?"

The astronaut – "That'd be nice. I'd like to share it."

The alien – "Maybe later."

Bringing the cocoa mug back to his seat, the explorer explores more visions: He senses the alien, a nocturnal creature (at least on land), often hides from predators. Whether on shore or in sea, she has to find hideaways like sea caves or thickets of mangroves to house her like a hut. But her sense of hearing, like the ears of prey, must not be lulled into a false sense of serenity; they must stay alert—any noise could be danger approaching like an eel lurking in a seabed. She is cautious around Earthlings, especially humans, the only species on this world known to smile while murdering, raping, stealing, and destroying. So, the homeless alien, who has about as much mass as a starfish, wades cautiously through this world, so as not to alert any beast of her presence. Suburbanites and urbanites and mansionites and trailerites are all capable of violence, just like submarines and torpedoes. Plus, the humans have connections to the law and make the laws—the alien doesn't—and they can easily have her shooed from *their* forest, or *their* lake, or anywhere else.

He wants to open the door for her, doesn't he, to let her in, but can he trust her?

As if knowing his thoughts:

The alien – "Like me, you grew up having to be able to read body gestures to save your hide, to know when someone was going to strike."

The astronaut – "Yeah, I've had meteorites hurl past me, but I'm used to stones being hurled at me. And my mother never cared about me getting hurt but only about me doing something that made me look stupid."

The alien – "I cared. I prayed for your safety. You once believed in prayer too. Science fiction was your childhood religion, a spiritual experience seeking life beyond Earth, something more beyond Terra, guardian *aliens*, if not guardian *angels*. You saw Mars as the ruby temple, a sanctuary, in the sky, where celestial monks prayed to our divine parents, God and God's mate."

The explorer moves a few rows down, getting closer to her. He seems hypnotized by her "trust me" tone to keep speaking.

The astronaut – "Unlike people, the stars seemed very dependable. They were always around each night. And much more accepting than the Hollywood stars who would come and go for parties."

The alien – "You could tell the stars in the sky anything with no fear of rejection. Is that why you're here tonight?"

The astronaut – "Mother is having a going-away party for me tonight. The bigtime publicist is always concerned about image, which my 'deformed' little sister couldn't live up to, and she died from … ? I don't know. Died from life? She was so young. Mother keeps that from the public."

The alien – "You can move closer if you like."

The astronaut moves inches into the darkness.

The alien – "That's enough for now."

The golden boy has been liked because of his looks and money, and she has *not* been liked because of her looks and lack of money, he senses.

The alien – "Please, finish what you were saying."

The astronaut – "Mother's angry I'm not there for the guests. I might be able to travel faster than the speed of sound but not faster than the speed of nagging. I'm leaving my mother's life forever. I said, 'Mother, I'll wave goodbye to you tomorrow from the platform.' She gave a thumbs up, 'See you on the jumbotron!' 'That's it?' I asked. And she sort of laughed. What more did I want?"

The alien – "Nothing jabs a heart more piercingly than a cold laugh."

The astronaut – "Yeah, I remember being about seven maybe, and I let my mother see my rock collection and…"

The alien – "She jabbed your heart with a sharp laugh. So, you eventually boarded up your fragile heart, and ignored the ache of loneliness, because it is too painful to deal with, and you've been avoiding a deep dive into the core to examine the range of that extensive, abysmal lonesomeness."

He shivers big and loud then hugs himself.

The astronaut – "God, you're right."

He keeps his arms around himself in a protective way.

The astronaut – "Most people would never suspect the playboy is lonely. Mother always makes sure various women are around me to craft the playboy image. Tabloids lie, imagine that. Scandalous lies sell magazines. Even when I was a kid, she made me go on dates and have big parties. Mother, herself, has started to believe the lies that I have a harem of bimbos. She doesn't care if I hurt a woman's feelings, only if I break one of the publicist's golden rules of ethics: 'Never screw over a reporter—they'll tell the world.' Well, I've never cared for the women, who welcome me into their beds and certainly want to welcome themselves into my wallet and spotlight. Those women never want to journey beyond the border above my pants; everything they want is in the pants region: wallet and their means to get my wallet. But mother is always backstage in my life, running the show, and my dad is back there, running her."

The alien – "Are your mother and father making you go on this mission?"

The explorer squints his eyes.

The astronaut – "The fact that they *want* me to go on this one-way mission is probably why I'm going, if that makes sense."

The alien – "It does to me. It's the same reason you like staying at the peaceful bed and breakfast, where the elderly lady, who runs it, seems so serene and godmotherly, along with her husband, both of them the picture of wedded bliss like God and God's mate on Earth, serving hot chocolate and apple dumplings and stories around the fireplace for weary travelers."

The astronaut – "I admit I always wanted a home as cozy as pancakes and Vermont syrup. Hot fresh chocolate pie cooling on the windowsill. I saw those images from old Hollywood and knew they weren't real, but the mythic cozy home wasn't unachievable—it could be achieved, not outside human reach. It's there at Chocolate Truffle Inn."

Mid-way down the theater, the astronaut shakes his head, like snapping out of a spell that made him spill his guts.

The astronaut – "Have you been stalking me since I was a kid?"

The alien – "Stalking? I've kept up with you, at the distance you keep up with the stars. The best I can with my failing sight and limited access to this world's news and goings-on. I sometimes use a magnifying glass to read the stories about you that wash up on shore. But stalking… is that how you describe that moment…when we saw each other in the sea?"

If hearts could explode, his would now, like a firecracker sparkling all across him.

The astronaut – "It's *you*?"

The alien – "Deep inside, you've known who I am since you called out from the stage, 'Is someone out there?' You knew who made the radio message for you all along, Captain Elvin. How could I know of that enchanting encounter if I, too, had not lived it?"

The astronaut – "You could've read the article I wrote about the sea creature."

The alien – "Please don't let your skepticism solidify into a wall between us. All these years, I've stayed by the inhospitable shore, in the cold, rough waters, just to encounter you again."

The astronaut – "Why did you swim away from me?"

The alien – "The same reason you didn't pursue me to the depths. Even though we're endowed with intuition, we feared it was wishful thinking to believe we would accept each other. Maybe the fear of rejection is a greater chasm than all of time and space between soulmates. Maybe the dread of being labeled insane for believing in soulmates is the greatest antagonist in love stories. But please believe me, I'd tear open the universe to find you. Would you rip the fabric of spacetime like unwrapping a gift to find me inside? Or is that wishful thinking?"

The astronaut (his boyhood voice gushing out) – "No, I've always wanted to find *her*. The first time I saw her, I felt, 'Her love is my fireplace.' But is it really you?"

The alien – "Yes, but I don't know of any way to prove I am *her* that is up to the scientist's standards. You will just have to trust your feelings. Did I laugh at or hold roughly any of your confessions tonight?"

The astronaut – "No."

The alien – "Even though I'm afraid too, I felt I must be the first to come to the surface if we are to embrace before the end. Please, come to me, my old friend, before I die."

On the word "die," something breaks inside him; something fragile like the hope for forever.

The astronaut – "Die?"

The alien – "Yes, while you're traveling the heavens, I'll be traveling to Heaven, hopefully."

As the explorer treks the darkness, *she* comes into light, as bared and scared as a delicate creature without its seashell, washed ashore in a foreign land. A big, bulky, breathing apparatus is attached to her tiny neck; over the throat area, the apparatus is equipped with a tiny plug, which must have been what dropped to the floor earlier and caused her labored breathing, and the sailor senses there is big, bulky, diving gear in the knapsack too, which the celestial mermaid uses to swim in Earth's unwelcoming sea. Her extraordinary face looks designed by Picasso. No symmetry. One large black Roswell eye droops; the other pale blue eye looks dead, as if it was killed by seeing too many heinous sights on the pale blue world. The bald creature has no nose, just flat skin, amphibiously slippery, the color of Jupiter. Clothing seems unnatural on her. Her two, long, side appendages, extending from her slim chest, end in mitts. No human has ever fully traveled her by eye or caress, a fact radiating from her severely isolated being, although by the tattered looks of the shawl, wild humans have grabbed at the alien out of curiosity and exploitation. All those traits considered "neat" on aliens—extra legs, antennae, three eyes, etc.—are not prized by humanity but labeled "malformations."

Whether she is a nonstandard human or from another planet—either way, she is an alien. Just like him. They don't belong on Earth; they're stranded on Terra. His mind is shaped differently from other Earthling's, her body is shaped differently, and their hearts are shaped similarly to one another's.

The creature appears to have legs, so maybe she wore a fluorescent fin all those years ago in the sea, or maybe the mermaid's fin turns into legs when she's on land. The mariner doesn't know for sure. Where's her pink hair and playful spirit? Why has she changed so much through the years? Because life on Earth has waged war on her? Isn't her battered body proof of the battle? A continuing battle. No wonder she desires a home inhabited by angels. Each wrestled breath takes her closer to her future home, but not yet at Heaven's welcome mat, here she is.

The alien – "I don't want you to see me as a diamond in the rough whose polishing is your task, but as a diamond in the rough whose roughness is your treasure."

Sitting in the chair beside her, the astronaut dips his fingers under his shirt and pulls out the raw chunk of unpolished diamond he wears on a necklace.

The astronaut – "This is the gift I wanted to travel across time to give to the lonely poet who left poems in the discarded music box."

When a tear buds from her dark eye, because even aliens feel and cry, he welcomes her in his arms, open wide enough to embrace the whole oddity of her, and she returns the embrace, swaddling all of his "okay" body, perfect to her.

Nestling, whispering, "I've missed you, I've missed you," he notices she also smells like oatmeal and honey, like they are mates from the same planet.

"After being in this warm nest you've built for me between your arms, all the winds of all the worlds will forever touch me as strangers," she says.

"I feel the same."

The cloth pouch sits in her lap, and he knows the Neptune-blue orb is inside. Now they no longer have to talk through words. While she's been stranded on Terra, she's held onto the blue orb as her home planet, because the blue symbolizes his eyes, and the red string tied around the sphere represents the red thread of destiny. She could show him the orb as tangible proof that she is *her*, but he trusts who she is on his heart's word.

Telepathically, they wonder, as the clock keeps ticking, "Maybe we've been brave with life, willing to risk it in outer space or death, because it has not been much of a life, but real bravery is this, what we're doing now—"

He peers into her multi-colored eyes.

And she peers into his blue, where the curtains have been lifted.

Now the fog parts, allowing their mate to dive deeply into the seas of each other's beings, where the light is on for everything to be seen.

Kissing, astronaut and alien merge.

Yearning satiated.

Outwardly and inwardly holding each other, their wished-for gift of togetherness, they see stars twinkling like Christmas lights strung in the frosted night sky, and the crescent moon shimmering like a flame in a menorah, and the celestial matchmaker smiles, in this beautiful universe of theirs, where the cocoa is hot and peppermint, and carols ring, and phantastic gene Z flourishes like snowflakes during the holidays, and the hidden bond between The Wedded Islets may get bent across years and lightyears, but it never tears, no more than light can tear—that's the way it goes in this holiday tale I'm telling about the astronaut and the alien.

Unfortunately, their story has not turned out this romantic way in life, in this universe, not yet. Wherever the astronaut truly is, I try, from my world, to send him dreams of "what if"—what if it were possible that if you and I were separated across all of time and space, we could find each other, just to love one another, if only we would brave the journey? I hope to warm him through telepathy, to tug on the red thread of fate to remind him of my existence and our bond, to tell him he's not so far away from romance and friendship as appears, while he's alone and cold in space, achy and homesick with no access to communication other than dreams and intuition. I even try to send him dreams of hot chocolate and apple dumplings, cozy cabins, crackling fireplaces, all the fixings of that special season on Earth known as the Holidays. I wish fate will sail him to my shore one night before it's too late, and we'll swim together in a softer sea. But maybe the character I've written here is just a dream, wishful thinking, and nothing like the real him at all.

Yours truly could be his dream, while the explorer is traveling the infinite unknown and dreaming of an alien who would yearn for him so much, she'd write their encounter into existence, so he could explore her world, *their* shared world, and she'd immortalize him in a love story, and to *her*, his name would be a synonym for friend…

Or another possibility: maybe we're characters in some other lonely soul's tale, some lonesome being's dream, a sole mind dreaming up friendship and romance and holiday magic to assuage its loneliness, and giving the characters an ability to dream within the dream to ease their own lonesomeness…

Good heavens, a lovelier possibility: maybe we're sharing this mysterious dream Life, two mates, sleeping side by side in our starboat's astral cabin, two best friends who have gotten so lost in the dream of separation, so enchanted with playing hide-n-seek in the constellations, we've forgotten the truth of togetherness—that we've been right beside each other all along, that before going to sleep, into this adventure Life, we gave each other a piece of ourselves, a droplet of our divine light, to keep inside like pearls, that we are all lockets of love—and it doesn't matter if we waste time apart in the world of matter, in this little play, because upon awakening we kids of starlight have eternity together in our warm home, reality, where the hearth never burns out…

I know one thing for certain—I know what the astronaut seeks in space: that *singularities* is not a contradiction, are not a contradiction. That's what the alien seeks too. I saved a few of my last breaths to light this pagefire for other star sailors, seeking the same in the sea of solitude, to warm themselves by—at least you're not alone in the search. Maybe the mermaid will even contact *him* through these words, shyly but bravely sailing across the cosmic ocean to give him a gift…

www.ingramcontent.com/pod-product-compliance
Lightning Source LLC
La Vergne TN
LVHW052051160826
845678LV00015B/3174
* 9 7 9 8 9 8 5 5 1 7 0 8 8 *